A Far Place in Time

LEE CROSS

A Far Place in Time

Virginia City Publishing
P. O. Box 51389
Sparks, NV 89435

Copyright © 2006, 2007
Leland W. Cross

ISBN: 0-9787596-0-5
ISBN: 978-0-9787596-0-5

Cover Design: George Foster
Interior Design: Desktop Miracles, Inc.

Printed in the United States of America

Publisher's Cataloging-in-Publication
(Prepared by The Donohue Group, Inc.)

Cross, Lee (Leland W.)
    A far place in time / Lee Cross.
        p. ; cm.
    ISBN-13: 978-0-9787596-0-5
    ISBN-10: 0-9787596-0-5
    1. Time travel—Fiction.   2. Historical fiction.   3. Science fiction.   I.
Title.
PS3603.R67 F37   2007

                                                                    813/.6

ACKNOWLEDGEMENTS

I wish to acknowledge the contribution of George Canady, the founder of the U.S. Merchant Marine Museum in Anderson, Indiana. Both George and his brother served in the U.S. Merchant Marine in World War II. Merchant seaman suffered the highest casualty rates of any branch of the service during that war. The lifeline provided by the Merchant Marine, not only supplied our troops but also kept Britain and the Soviet Union alive. Mr. Canady's technical assistance was invaluable to me and I can't thank him enough.

DISCLAIMER

Much of the adventure in this story has a basis in historical fact. Nevertheless, dialogues representing actual conversations between real life historical figures in this story are for the most part fictional. Something like them might have actually taken place because of the nature of the event, but none of these are direct quotes.

PROLOGUE

I, John Lander, know I must die soon. I may not last until sunset. All I can do from here is look out the window of this hospital room. My breath doesn't come easy; this pneumonia is incurable. I would be dead now if it were not for this oxygen tent. My best friend just left me. Strange, his body is wasted with lung cancer; yet he will outlive me.

I need to get this story off my chest. Where is my son? He said he was coming. Where is he? I don't have long. I now turn my head to the sound of the door opening. Finally, I see him there walking into my room.

"Hello, Dad!"

> *"Time is an illusion that has purpose"*
>
> EDGAR CAYCE

chapter

1

ADRIFT

My head nodded to the rhythm of the waves as I slowly woke up. I had been drifting in and out of sleep constantly. Now the sun was rising to midmorning above the horizon and was burning through my eyelids. The memory came back to me, the shuddering of the ship, the muffled explosion of the torpedoes, the yells, the men running back and forth, and the confusion.

I had been shaken out of my makeshift bed on the port side of the boat deck by the sound of two torpedoes striking the Roderick. I didn't look at my pocket watch, but I knew it happened just minutes after seven bells that evening. They hit us on the starboard side straddling the number two hold. It began to flood. This was quickly followed by two more torpedoes also hitting us forward. I could feel the Roderick going down by the bow. The call to abandon ship came over the loudspeaker.

My lifeboat station was the number four boat on the starboard side; I quickly ran there, and joined the others in swinging out the davits to lower the boat. I didn't know where Mack or Leo were. Within minutes, two more torpedoes slammed into the starboard side. One hit the engine room; the other hit the number three hold.

This last impact threw me and other men working those starboard boats into the water. A large splash took place not far from me. It was the wooden hatch cover from the number three hold. The explosion in that hold had popped it out and into the drink. I gasped for air as my head broke the surface. I desperately swam to it and managed to heave myself on top. It was designed to float and could be used as emergency life raft for one man. Incredibly, the ship was still moving away from me. This would be my salvation.

The engine room was flooding. A boiler exploded. The Roderick came to a standstill. She was going down fast and the ship wouldn't last much longer. Then, the rear half righted itself temporarily, as the bow section forward of the number three hold broke off and sank. There were still men on deck. This allowed them to swing another boat over the port side. As the number three hold and the engine room flooded, the Roderick made her final death plunge as her stern turned upward with the propeller shaft almost vertical to the water. The displaced and cascading water swamped that last life boat on the port side. As the ship disappeared beneath the waves she dragged many of the men down with her. From start to finish, it took the Roderick less than twenty minutes to sink.

Fortunately, we had taken on several extra life rafts at Capetown. They were stacked on deck to accommodate the soldiers we had also taken on board there. These floated away as the ship sank. Shaped like a doughnut with rims of balsa wood bound together with canvas webbing, six by four feet, they were virtually unsinkable. There was a lattice, bound together with rope in the middle which provided support for a man's feet. They were designed so that no matter which side landed in the water, they would always be right side up. I abandoned the hatch cover and swam to the nearest one.

Already, several other men were making their way to it. I heard splashing nearby and a cry for help. The seaman blindly flailed the water. Paddling with my hands, I tried to maneuver the raft toward the wounded man. His head was barely out of the water when our fingers touched. He desperately groped for the raft. "Please help me," he cried. With a final heave I reached him and grabbed the man by his arm and shoulder. With difficulty, I slowly pulled his heavy weight into the raft. The man had been badly burned, and he was covered with oil. Other men were clambering into the raft by now. I cradled the injured man's head as I wiped oil from his eyes with my fingers. He opened them and looked up at me. "Johnny," he said.

"Milo, is that you?"

He nodded his head slightly. I tried to comfort him as best as I could. But his pain from the burns he received when the boiler ruptured was intense. He had been in the engine room when the torpedoes hit, and was the only man able to get out. He grasped my arm for reassurance. "Johnny, I was always wonderin', did you do something to them dice, that first time in Pedro?"

"Yeah, Milo," I confessed. "Just concentrate on living now; I'll make it up to you later."

"I don't reckon so, Johnny. My times almost come and I'm goin' to do some answerin' soon myself."

"Don't talk nonsense, Milo, you're alive. You're going to be alright."

Our situation in the balsa raft was bleak. It was overloaded with men. Some were halfway in the water. Two of them were badly injured. Besides Milo, there was a Navy boy from the forward three inch gun. He had been thrown into the water from the impact of the second set of torpedoes. He had a massive head injury and was mercifully unconscious. His Kapok had kept him afloat and we pulled him into the raft. The mules and donkeys corralled on deck were becoming a problem. Those in the bow section that managed to swim away from the Roderick, were floundering in the water, and braying in terror. Some of them desperately tried to climb onto our raft, and we had to beat them off for our own survival. I felt a sinking feeling of remorse as I had to repeatedly kick one of the poor horrified animals in its head. It desperately tried to claw its hooves into our raft. These animals nearly upset us several times. Within the next hour, they finally became exhausted; until, one by one, they drowned.

Milo died in my arms that night. The poor sailor with the head injury died also. He never regained consciousness.

———

Milo, I remember that first night we met. I was on the run; running from what, I wasn't sure. Running to what, I didn't have a clue. But I knew I had to get out of Los Angeles. I remember looking at my watch that night two months ago, and thinking, where to now, John Lander? I went back to the red car stop and caught another car. It was going to San Pedro. That was fine with me. I had no plan and no prospects. But I knew I had to become someone else, establish another identity, become a chameleon and blend into new surroundings. One thing for certain, I could no longer pretend to be John Winters. In San Pedro, I got off the red car and started walking aimlessly. It was dark and getting cold. I saw a bar. I fingered the loose coins in my pockets, mostly silver dollars. They were heavy and jingled as I walked. Imagine, these coins were supposed to bring me wealth. But here, they are just silver dollars! I decided to have a drink. It might be my last on this side of a set of iron bars.

I walked in and looked around. The place was mostly filled with sailors, both merchant seaman and Navy boys along with some longshoremen. I went to the bar and sat down on a vacant stool. I sat there and stared at the glass of bourbon in front of me. I was lost in thought, until I became aware of a man standing next to me. His hands were pressed together as he leaned on the bar, his head slightly bent. I could tell he wanted a drink and didn't have the means to buy one. I felt like an island, all alone. I had need for human conversation. "Hello," I said. "How's it going?"

The man slowly turned his head, and furled his brows. "Not so very good, you see. I was just being cleaned out in a crap game."

"How about a drink?" I asked. The little man brightened up immediately, and I asked the bartender to bring him a beer.

He offered me his hand. "Leo McGinty is the name," he said in his distinctive Irish accent. He was a short man, fifty-ish, from Cork, Ireland. He had a gray beard that tapered in front. This, coupled with his alert blue eyes, gave him a striking appearance as he spoke. Leo immediately opened up with lively conversation. He was a merchant seaman, and was serving on a newly commissioned Liberty Ship. It was in the process of taking on ammunition from the army terminal warehouses along the pier in San Pedro. He told me its destination was someplace in the South Pacific, but he didn't know where. As we got acquainted, I ordered more drinks for us, and had the bartender set him up with a shot of Irish whiskey.

"Tell me more about this crap game, Leo?"

"Well," he said, "Me and some of the boys were playing in the back room. There's this fellow from our ship, Milo, you see. And he was taking us all pretty steady, but slow like. He's an oiler on the black gang of the Roderick. He doesn't roll for himself. He takes us all on and waits for us to seven out. Not always, you see, but usually he does most of the winnin' of the money."

"You mean he plays the dark side, Leo?"

"What's the dark side?" he asked.

"He's playing the same as the house, Leo. But in alley craps he has the advantage. Neither the two nor the twelve are barred against him, as it would be for a man playing the dark side in a casino. He gets to play just as the house does, which gives him about a one and a half per cent advantage over a right bettor."

"What's a right bettor?" Leo asked.

"You, me, anyone who wants to make the point. Those that don't want the point to pass are called wrong bettors."

A stocky, sturdy looking guy walked up next us and glared at me. He put his hand on Leo's shoulder. "Leo, I'm going back to the ship. Wanna go?"

"Mack, I'll just be having some drinks with me new friend here." Leo turned to me and paused. "What is your name, mister?" he asked.

It was certain I couldn't still be John Winters. I considered, why not be myself until something comes to mind. "I'm John Lander."

Mack took my hand in a bone crushing grip. He nodded to me. "Mack Porter. Leo, are you comin'?"

Leo frowned, "Mack, let's not be hasty. We're having a fine bit of fun here now. How about a beer for yourself?"

"I'm taking my last twenty back to the ship, Leo. But maybe I'll have one beer."

I looked back at Leo. "Tell me more about this crap game."

"Ask Mack here; he lasted longer than I did."

I turned my attention to Mack as he spoke. "Yeah, Milo is still cleanin' up back there. I don't think the game will go on much longer."

"Mack, do you think you can get me into that game?" I asked.

"Sure! I'll do that for you. You don't look or talk like a cop. Come on."

The three of us walked into the back room. "Mack, did you say you still have a twenty?" I asked.

"Yeah!"

"Bet as I do. Don't take the dice; pass them to me. Maybe we can spoil Milo's day after all." Craps had been a passion of mine, before I got hooked on the horses. But here I knew what I was doing. Well enough in fact, to have been thrown out of three casinos in Nevada, and photographed in a few more. No, I wasn't a cheat, not in the usual sense anyway. But I had learned the art of setting the dice, which combined with the correct flick of the wrist, could alter the odds in my favor. This was called the blanket roll. The big question was, would Milo or anybody else know what I was doing? I knew this technique was around before the First World War, but I could only guess how well it was known in 1945. My mentor in the game had been my own uncle, my dad's younger brother. He was the black sheep of the family, and he was my favorite uncle. Dad always said I was too much like my Uncle Lonnie. The blanket roll couldn't be used in the casinos in my time. They were on to this trick. The table rails were lined with rubber spikes to prevent its use. Still, casinos wouldn't tolerate anyone trying it on them as I had done.

We walked into the back room. It was dimly lit, with a scattering of tables and chairs and filled with smoke. Against one wall a few men were huddled. I was in luck. They were shooting on a rug, probably to spare the dice from getting chipped on the hard floor.

The shooter had just sevened out as we walked up. Mack spoke to the rather mean looking man picking up the bet. "Milo, this is John here. He wants to get in the game. He's OK."

Milo just looked at me and nodded. I reached into my pocket and pulled out my silver dollars and a few small bills. Milo passed the dice to me. "Milo, can I take the odds? I asked.

"No," he replied.

"OK, hotshot; it's your call."

Milo glared at me. "You callin' me names? I'll kick your ass!"

Mack held up his palm toward him. "Easy, Milo; it ain't nothin.'"

"It burns me, Mack. I don't like it when some stranger gets cutesy with me."

Leo whispered in my ear. "Johnny, Milo's got a short fuse."

"Sorry, Milo. I didn't mean anything by it."

No odds! Well, this would take longer. But I would grind him down. I set the dice as I picked them up. No one took notice of what I was doing. Then I gave them the blanket roll. There was no look of recognition on anyone's face. This would be easier than I thought. Three hours later I had over seven hundred dollars in front of me. Mack had a stack of bills in front of him too. I sevened out sometimes, sure! But I made my points far more often than this happened. No one knew what I was doing. Everybody was having a good time, everybody except Milo. He had become sullen as he steadily stared at me. I was glad this wasn't a back alley with just him and me in it.

Finally, he exploded. "You're cheatin'!"

"How, Milo?"

"I don't know; but you're cheatin'!" He stood up and took a step toward me.

In a blink, Mack jumped between us and stared him down. I could see that Milo was intimidated by him. Over the next few months, I would find out why. Milo stepped back. Mack turned to me. "Games over!" he said harshly.

The tension in the air relaxed as Leo grabbed me and Mack by the arm. "Johnny, me boy, let's you, me and Mack here get a drink."

We went back into the bar. I gave Leo fifty dollars. "For you, you deserve it." The little man brightened up and eagerly took the money.

Mack purposely sat between me and Leo. After our drinks were brought, he turned to me and smiled. "I don't know what you were doin'. But I know you did something. You never shook them dice after you picked 'em up. Am I right?"

"Could be. Not complaining are you? Make out OK?"

"Yeah! Up three hundred! What's your gig, John?"

I didn't feel like stringing him out with long lie that I might not remember later on. "I just want to disappear for a while."

"On the run?"

"Maybe."

"From what?"

These questions wouldn't go away unless I threw him off the trail. "I have two wives, Mack, and I got caught. I don't want to go to jail. I need to become someone else for a while and think things out."

Mack smiled at me. He liked that answer. "Maybe I can help you. Stick with me."

Leo and I drank ourselves into near oblivion before the bar closed. That wasn't Mack's style. He sipped slow and steady. They checked me in to a seedy hotel near the waterfront. I remembered Mack saying he would be back for me in the morning.

It was early, not quite seven. I awoke to loud knocking on the door of my tiny room. With a pounding head, I groped toward the door and opened it. Mack was standing there in front of me. He looked as fresh as if he'd never had a drink just those few hours before.

"Come on, Johnny." He threw a sea bag at my feet. "We have business and gotta move fast."

"What business, Mack?" I reached for my pounding head.

"You want to disappear don't you? Well, here's your chance. One of the able seamen from our ship got into a fight yesterday. This was before we met up. He hurt a guy pretty bad, and it looks like he's gonna be in jail for long time. I'll get you put in his place, but we gotta move fast. The Roderick goes out at nine."

"Mack, I don't know anything about ships, or the Merchant Marine. Hell, I don't even have any papers!"

He squinted his brown eyes as he smiled at me. Then, reached into the inner pocket of his sea coat and pulled out some papers. "This Z Card belonged to my old shipmate, Johnny Grady. He didn't have any family except for a sister in New York. When he died in the hospital some months ago, I was with him. He gave everything he had to me, which didn't amount to anything much. But I didn't throw these away. I figured I might look up his sister someday, and give them to her. Trouble is; I don't know her married name."

Mack handed the paper to me. I unfolded the full sheet sized paper and saw the photo of a bearded sailor on it. It identified John Grady, a Merchant Marine Seaman. "Come on, Johnny. I gotta get you to the hiring hall quick before that spot is filled. I know the union man there. He owes me a favor. But we can't waste no time."

"Is this paper all I need, Mack? Don't they do background checks or something?"

"Are you kiddin'? They're screamin' for every living body they can get. And once you get your Z Card, why would you want anything else?"

"I don't even have suitable clothes."

"Don't worry, Johnny; I got you fixed up. Grady's sea bag was still at his old lady's house, the one he used to shack with when he was in town. I caught hell gettin' that broad up this mornin'. But I got it right here; see! He was about your size. Put on these duds and forget about your fancy suit. So let's get goin'."

On the way to the hiring hall I learned that Mack was the Bosun on the Roderick. As an able seaman, I would be working directly under him. John Grady was just a little older than me. The photo of him wasn't that good, and he had a beard. I might be able to fake it if the Z Card wasn't examined too closely. He was born in Galway, Ireland, but had lived in New York since he was five. Good, I didn't have to fake an Irish accent.

Mack did know the union boss in the hiring hall. This part wasn't easy. As I soon learned, the National Maritime Union was tightly controlled. It was the largest and most powerful of the mariner's unions. A seaman would turn in his card and have to wait until his turn came up. Mack took the union boss aside. I could see them talking but couldn't hear what they said. The union man shook his head several times. Mack didn't let up, and then passed him something. I guessed it was money. I was moved around other men who stood for the job. He hurried me on board the ship. Thirty minutes later, I signed the articles as they were placed before me by the purser in the officer's mess. I tried to make sense of what had happened to me. This is crazy! I, John Lander, am a seaman in the Merchant Marine in a war twenty-six years before I was born! The FBI is after me! And I got the worst goddamn hangover I can remember!

San Pedro Harbor was crowded with these new Liberty Ships, all in some stage of progress, taking on their various cargoes. The Roderick was one of these, built right here in San Pedro. With a thirty-six man crew, she carried a 4.5 inch gun on the stern; a 3.5 inch gun on the bow and eight twenty millimeter Oerlikon anti-aircraft guns placed in elevated gun tubs spaced around the ship, four forward and four aft. We had a contingent of twenty-four Navy boys to man the guns. They were under the command of a ninety day-wonder.

Our destination was Calcutta. We had a load of bombs destined for the 58th Bomb Wing, operating from bases near that city. They were steadily pounding the Japs in Burma with their B-29s from Kharagpur and other locations around Calcutta.

There was a delay in our initial movement. But shortly after nine, the harbor tugs were nudging the Roderick out of the army ammunition terminal. She took her place in queue, waiting for the convoy to depart. And I was with her!

chapter

2

SURVIVE

s the sun broke over the horizon, I came out of my stupor and became aware of things around me. I began to acutely feel pain in my limbs and neck from the exertion just a few hours before. At daybreak, we committed their bodies to the sea. Jackson, the ship's cook, recited the Lord's Prayer over them. The hot sun would have rapidly started decomposing these bodies. I was naked from the waist up, so I kept the Navy boy's blood soaked jumper to cover my upper body. Those final few words said over them was all we could do.

Fortunately, the chain connecting the leather pouch holding my Z Card to my belt was intact. And remarkably, I still had all of my money in my pockets. Mack warned me about keeping it in the ship's safe while we were still in Capetown. "Don't trust nobody with your money, Johnny, especially the ship's captain."

Staying dry was impossible. Water seeped up through the lattice under our feet and splashed over the sides. My pocket watch was soaked with sea water and no longer worked. Even with Milo and the Navy boy gone, the raft was still overcrowded. Unlike the rigid 25 man rafts and the one surviving lifeboat, these balsa rafts had no water or food. That first night we drifted apart from most other survivors. By the first daybreak, there was only one other balsa raft in sight. Using our hands, all men from both rafts paddled until we were together. The other wasn't as overloaded. Two of our men transferred over to it. A seaman on the other one had saved his coat. We shredded it with a pocket knife. Then we tied these strips together forming a crude rope, enabling us to lash the two rafts together. At least we wouldn't drift apart. Together, we made a larger object for our rescuers to see.

Many years would pass, before I would learn the full story behind the Roderick's sinking. Only two of the large rigid rafts were ever recovered. One lifeboat from the port side survived. The other had been swamped when the ship's rear section made its death plunge. Neither of the starboard life boats made it into the water. The third set of torpedoes disrupted their launching. At least six of the balsa rafts contained survivors. They weren't all as overloaded as ours.

We had been torpedoed by a German submarine, which wasn't supposed to exist in the Indian Ocean. It was part of a squadron transferred to the Far East, because the Germans knew the allies wouldn't expect it. We didn't know at that time, but our plight was worsened because no emergency radio message had been sent. It would be days before our disappearance was noticed. Our radio officer, the third mate, was never recovered.

And this would always remain a mystery to the survivors of the Roderick. Captain McIver went down with his ship.

Losing any sense of time over these next two days, I drifted in and out of sleep. The constant immersion with salt water chaffed our skins. It was impossible to stay dry. All of us slumped and rested as best we could. The tropical sun pounded us mercilessly during the day, as our condition continued to worsen. All I could think about was water. We sometimes saw distant smoke, just over the horizon. Their lookouts couldn't see us. An occasional distant sail from some dhow would sometimes appear. Again, no one saw us. But we were spared bad weather; our luck in this held steady. At night, the stars glittered brightly over us as the wind brushed the clouds aside and somewhat cooled our agony.

At the dawn of what must have been the third daybreak, a sudden jolt tossed our raft upward; I heard a bloodcurdling scream. It was Banty, the cook's helper. In the still dim early light he was holding his stump of a right arm and screaming with pain. In our crowded raft, his right arm had slumped into the water when he fell asleep. A shark took it off six inches above the wrist. This was really bad. The shark had tasted blood and soon there were several more visible in the water around us. A sailor took off his belt and put a tourniquet on Banty's arm. There was very little more we could do for him, except cover his stump with a sweat and salt water soaked undershirt. As the sun rose higher, we could see more of them circling the rafts. None of us had any medical experience. I believe I would have traded all of my ill gotten gains at that moment for just one dose of morphine to ease poor Banty's pain. Finally, I brought the matter up before the other men. "We have to do something about that wound. He is going to get gangrene and die if we don't."

Jackson spoke first. "There ain't much we can do, Johnny, except just hope we get picked up soon."

I was pensive for a while; something deep in my memory was trying to surface. I tried to remember. When I was a boy, my dad had encouraged me to take a survival course when I was in the scouts. What was that I read about primitive cures? What was it? Yes! Now I remember! "Can any of you men pee? Even a little?" I repeated myself, and gained their attention. In spite their dehydration, a couple of them said yes. "Look here, men; urine contains ammonia. Primitive people would sometimes urinate on each other's wounds to disinfect them. Ammonia kills germs."

They looked skeptical. But I was able to convince them it was Banty's only chance. Jackson and another man held him down while those two men performed the task, even though it was only a slight trickle. Another man produced a handkerchief which we soaked in urine. With this, we bandaged him as best we could; and put Banty in the center of the raft. We all took turns holding his stub upward to keep it as dry as possible and stop the bleeding.

The sharks stayed with us until early afternoon, when they dispersed as a school of dolphins swam by. Sensing our plight, these wonderful animals stayed with us for a long time. It was amazing! They showed more humanity toward us than we did to ourselves. Everyone became steadily weaker and severely sunburned wherever our skin was exposed. My lips were cracked and parched. I could see the eyes of my shipmates were becoming sunken and I knew mine must be the same. The least movement of my lips was painful. My mouth and tongue had never been so dry and my saliva was thick.

Time! It was the one thing I still had plenty of, time to think about what went wrong. Hank, what the hell happened? No one could have predicted this outcome in ten thousand years. Was it fate; or were we just playthings of the Almighty? But, we were going to be so careful; attend to every detail. Where did we go astray?

On March 14th, we had our first stroke of luck. We were spotted by a Liberator with British markings combing the area for survivors. They wagged their wings in recognition and then made a second low level pass. They dropped us a packet which landed about a hundred yards away, and then bobbed in the water as it surfaced. The Liberator then flew off toward the east, toward Colombo.

We knew our ordeal would end soon. Using our hands, we tried without success to paddle the rafts over to the floating packet. Looney pulled off his shoes off. "I've had enough of this," he said. He jumped in, covered the distance to the packet, and then swam back, nudging it ahead of him. We pulled it inside and shared the contents among both rafts. It contained cans of spam, crackers, water, bandages and cigarettes with matches. This last part was especially appreciated by the other men. After we satisfied our craving for water, each of us opened a can of spam. We devoured these. I only had my fingers to scoop out the meat. It didn't matter. This didn't taste like anything I ever bought at a five star restaurant. It was better! The lessons from these days would never be forgotten. I learned the meaning of the words hunger and thirst.

In late afternoon, we saw a seaplane coming toward us from the eastern horizon. Within minutes, though it seemed more like hours, a Mark I Walrus with Royal British Navy markings was bouncing across the waves toward us. It came almost right up to the rafts. Soon, the door opened up and a crewman threw us a line. We grabbed it and the British airman pulled our rafts up to the door. The Brit standing in the hatchway first greeted and then gave us the bad news. "We can't carry this many now, mates. We have to take the worst cases from both rafts first. We're from a Royal Navy Cruiser not four hours sailing time from here. They'll pick up the rest of you blokes straight away at first light tomorrow morning. Those men staying behind must get into the same raft. We want you all together. We can't have you blokes drifting apart."

None of us were happy about being left behind. But there was nothing else the British flyers could do. Though designed for air sea rescue and patrol work, this shagboat couldn't carry us all, not two full raft loads of seamen. These planes were mainly used for recon work and rescuing downed pilots. We passed Banty up first, he would live. Four of us had to stay behind and wait for the cruiser. Compared to some of the others, I was still in pretty good shape; so I was one of them, along with Looney and Jackson from our raft. Alabam joined us from the other one. The Brit also left us a flare gun to signal the cruiser tomorrow morning. We tied it to a balsa log. The British Flyer shoved our raft off. "Chins up, mates, we're off to the ship. You'll get picked up soon; early tomorrow just like I said." The seaplane revved up its engines and lumbered through the waves, bouncing erratically. It almost looked like it wasn't going to lift up, but then it slowly climbed out of the water. We watched it pass out of sight.

Jackson wanted to cut the other raft loose. Alabam was against this idea. "It ain't hurtin' nothin,' Jackson. We might need it; leave it be." He was right!

We hoped the flyer was wrong. Maybe that cruiser would get here before dark settled in around us. We strained our eyes toward the horizon. It was would soon be dark. Thirty, not more than forty minutes later, Looney yelled. "Look there, boys! A periscope! We're gonna get picked up by a submarine. How did they get here so fast?" The form continued to emerge from the wake of foam it created as it broke surface.

"They didn't get here that fast," I said to the others. "That sub captain must have seen the seaplane touch down. Now he's coming up for a look." Less than two hundred yards from us, the large metallic mass straightened up as it finished emerging from the waves. I looked at the markings on its hull. "Boys, this is going to get ugly. That's a Jap sub. They'll kill us."

"You're right, Johnny; this is real bad," Looney added. "They don't want us to get back on another ship."

We were in a tight spot. The Japs began coming on deck. I could see them mounting a machine gun on the side facing us. "Over the side, boys, quick!" I yelled. I dove head first into the water on the side opposite the sub. The others followed me, but they still had their Kapok life jackets on. Their heads were bobbing on the surface. Under the water I could hear the plinking of bullets as they hit the water and the screams of my shipmates. I went deeper as I felt the rush of water from the impact of bullets coming close to me. I could hear the sound of the sub's diesel engine getter louder. They had turned into us. The rafts would be rammed. Desperately, I swam away from them under the waves, as fast as I could to escape the impact. The sound from the propeller filled my ears and I could hear the rafts breaking up. I felt the tug from the sub's propeller trying to suck me in; but I was far enough away, and soon the sound of its rotating blades began to fade.

My lungs felt like they were going to explode; I couldn't stand it any longer. I slowly broke the surface and gasped for air. The diesel sounds steadily died out as the boat receded in the distance. Our raft was in splinters. The other one had not been hit directly, only grazed, but it was in fragments too. Two longer pieces of the balsa survived. They were about six feet long. Though nothing more than driftwood now, they still floated. I swam to the closer one, and kept it between me and the sub until they were out of sight. For I knew they would come back and finish the job if they saw me in the water. My shipmate's bodies had already sunk beneath the waves as their kapoks had been ripped apart by Japanese gunfire. My situation was desperate. There was blood all around me in the water. It was only a matter of time before the sharks showed up.

I heaved my body onto that fragment of balsa log, strad-dling it lengthwise. The other piece was nearby. I paddled my log belly board style over to it, and pulled it alongside me. I shifted my body over both, distributing my weight among them. Holding them together was a constant struggle. I had to use my hands and feet to keep them from drifting apart. This was complicated. They didn't rise and fall together; they reacted dif-ferently to the swell of waves. I was constantly deluged as the waves lapped over me, but that was the least of my problems. Another piece of driftwood gained my attention. Seeing the flare gun still strapped to it, I paddled over and retrieved it. I could use it to defend myself against the sharks. No! I must try to save it for tomorrow; it's my only chance. I untied the flare gun and stuffed inside the jumper next to my back.

Reality struck me. So this is how it goes. I'm going to die in the Indian Ocean twenty-six years before I was born. This would be the greatest fight I would ever face, trying to stay alive, just this one night. I need something to keep me going, a reason to keep struggling. I have one; it's Charmaine. If I could just see her one more time, touch her again, and kiss her pretty lips. At least you were mine for a while, Charmaine. Dig deep, Lander; think of Charmaine. She's worth living for. Remember! Remember the day you met Charmaine.

Darkness fell and I was aware of dark forms in the water, only inches away. Sharks periodically bounced off these fragments of driftwood. They sensed that I was there. Only inches of wood separated us. But they didn't like its feel. With a half hearted effort, any of them could have easily knocked me off; or for that matter, they could have risen underneath and parted the pieces of driftwood. Would these fragments be enough? Holding them together and remaining on top was a tricky balancing act. I was tired, and my hands were numb from the effort. A voice inside my head spoke to me; hold or die, Lander. If you relax, you're lost.

That night I relived my whole life. Images from my past flashed before me. Could I come to grips with all that has happened? I imagined my grandmother, the only one I remembered, begging me to hold on. The mind plays strange tricks. It can convince itself of anything. It is said that there are no atheists in combat. Well, there's none floating around in the Indian Ocean at 3:00 A. M. in the morning either. I wasn't a religious man; but here and now, I prayed for help.

Slowly light broke on the horizon. I vaguely knew my time was about up as I floated in and out of consciousness. Struggling to stay awake, it was difficult control my limbs. But then I had a dream. I saw smoke on the horizon. I was rum dumb punchy

as fatigue dulled my thoughts. What good does it do to dream?
Let go, Lander; let go and soon you'll be in a deep peaceful sleep
forever. Nothing else matters, Lander. Let go; just go to sleep.
But my dream wouldn't go away. The smoke was still there. Is it
smoke, Lander? No! It couldn't be; you're dreaming. Somehow,
I pulled out the flare gun and pointed it toward the sky. Would
it fire? It did!

My next memory was waking up in a small room. A man
walked over to me as I lay in bed. "'Ello, myte. I see yer comin
around," he said in his cheerful Cockney accent.

"Where am I?"

"Yer on one of his majesty's cruisers. And yer goin' to
Darwin on it, first class yer might say, right 'ere in the medical
ward."

"How long have I been here?"

"Myte, yer been asleep 'ere near on nineteen hours. Ow
'bout a cuppa tea?"

"Do you suppose I could get some coffee?" I asked.

"'Ere, I'll see what I can do, myte. Yer ship mytes are 'ere
from the plyne yesterday."

I became aware of the other men in the ward. Banty was in
a bed close by. Other friends were too. Before long, a doctor was
looking me over.

The British seamen took good care of us. They gave us
clothes to wear and we ate well. I slept and rested a lot. I actually
had sheets again. The skipper questioned me extensively about
the Jap Sub. "We'll settle with those bastards one day soon,
Seaman Grady." He further told me his orders would take this
ship directly to Darwin. We would be there in a few days. There
would be no stop over at Calcutta or Colombo.

I hoped the captain could give me news about my friends? I asked him if there were other survivors; he promised to inquire. Later that first morning, he sent me word that numerous survivors had been rescued by a second cruiser, but could give me no details. The other cruiser would be going to Darwin also, its destination before picking them up. This was encouraging; there was a chance. I had plenty of time to rest and think before we arrived in Darwin. Time to think about my friends, and most of all, Charmaine.

chapter

3

REFLECTIONS

O ver the next two days, I regained my strength and health. I had plenty of time to think as I relaxed on the British cruiser. I pondered those events that had brought me here, to a far place in time. I closed my eyes and remembered that fateful day sixty-two years from now. These reflections took me forward to that day in 2007 when I sat in my office in Corona Del Mar.

I picked up the ringing phone and placed it to my ear. "Hello?"

A young female voice spoke to me. "Lander?"

"Are you pretty? You sound pretty."

The girl giggled. "You never change. This is Sally. Ms. Randall would like to see you in her office right away. Can I tell her you're coming up?"

My mood soured as I heard the name Randall. I wondered why the creature from hell was calling for me. What have I done now? "Oh sure, Sally; I'm on the way!" I hung up the phone, stood up, cinched up my tie and put on my coat. Then I walked out of my office on the second floor of Bradshaw Investments International, into the elevator and up to the 4th floor.

As I approached her office suite, the executive director was walking out of Connie's office. "Ms Randall is expecting you, Lander," he said indifferently.

This doesn't look good. "Thank you, Charlie." I had only seriously spoken with Connie Randall a handful of times, none of them very pleasant. She was Quincy Bradshaw's daughter, early-thirties, fair good looks, a product of one of those eastern preppie schools and understandably divorced. She took over Quincy's duties when he went into retirement two years ago.

When did Connie last want to see me? I remember now. It was on a Friday, last month, when she called me in. "You are flirting too much with our female employees, Mr. Lander. That is unprofessional; it must stop immediately. It is a form of sexual harassment and we will not tolerate any of that at Bradshaw." Previous conversations with her had been almost as memorable.

I opened the door to the executive office and walked in. "Hi Sally."

The pretty girl behind the desk glanced at me. "Go right on in; Ms. Randall is expecting you."

I was overcome with curiosity as I walked by her. "Sally, we haven't talked since the New Year's Eve Party. Is your boyfriend still mad at me?"

Smiling, she looked up at me. "Go stuff yourself, John Lander!"

I walked into the sanctuary of the creature, trying to be cheerful. "Good day, Ms. Randall, what's on the agenda this morning?"

"Sit down, Lander!"

Great start I thought. She's either going to promote me or fire me. It was the latter.

"Mr. Lander, we are eliminating your position. I'm sure with your skill level, you will do quite well on the outside."

I knew this was so much bull. "Why have you always disliked me so, Ms. Randall?"

She leveled her cool grey eyes at me. "Mr. Lander, Bradshaw Investments International doesn't really need the full-time services of a net-working engineer. For periodic service, we can contract your duties to outside sources at a considerably smaller figure than your $96,000 per year salary, and eliminate a bonus too. However, knowing my father was fond of you, I asked for his approval first." She handed me an envelope. "There is three months severance pay here, Mr. Lander, which I personally think is too generous. But Quincy stipulated that you would receive that much."

"Quincy approved?" My jaw dropped. "Can I speak to him?"

"Quincy also said I would have to make the decisions as I saw fit. And if it came to this, I could do it my way! You'll be clearing your desk out within the hour I expect?"

"It won't take that long, Ms Randall."

"Good day, Mr. Lander."

I left without saying another word. I had known happier days when Quincy occupied this office.

As I walked out of the large front doors of the Mediterranean style building on the Pacific Coast Highway in Corona Del Mar, all I could think of was Quincy. We had met at Santa Anita back in '97. I had just gone through a cool 500 hundred dollars, and was contemplating whether to invest my last twenty at the bar, or on some other nag. Next, I was aware of this man standing next to me, in his early fifties, wearing an expensive three piece suit with a Rolex on his wrist worth more than my car.

"Having a good day?" he asked, as we watched the horses coming out of the paddock for the next race.

"Fair. I've had better," I lied.

Smiling, he replied, "I've got a good tip on Screaming Laura and Stormy Amy in the exacta. I think I'm going to bet something on them."

"They're both long shots, sir."

"Really! Doesn't that make it delightful?"

"Where are you going to watch the race from?" I asked.

"From the John Henry Room," he replied as he walked away.

I went inside the club house, and paused at the bar. Then I kept walking; hell, I'm a Celt at heart. This last twenty will only save my bacon if I play, and it won't fill my glass very long if I don't. I went to the window and laid my last twenty on a quinella with Screaming Laura and Stormy Amy. With a quinella, either horse could come in first and I would still win. I watched them from the clubhouse come over the line, one and two. Soon afterward, I was at the window. The quinella paid $425 on a $2 ticket and

I received ten payoffs. They withheld 20% and made me sign a tax form. I could scarcely contain my excitement! I wanted to see the old gentleman again, and maybe buy him a drink. He was my newest, greatest hero.

I went to the entrance of the John Henry Room, paid my ten bucks and went inside. He was sitting at a table with two friends, a cup of coffee and a shot of some liquor in front of him. He looked up at me as I approached. I stopped in front of him. "May I join you all for a drink?"

His companions stopped talking, waiting for him to reply. Smiling, he slowly nodded, and motioned for me to take a seat. "What is your name, sir?"

"John Lander. Just call me Lander, everybody does."

The old gentleman gestured to each of his friends. "Mr. Lander; my colleagues, Jim Lerner and David Johnson, and I am Quincy Bradshaw."

The other two men rose, shook my hand saying, "Pleased to meet you," almost in unison.

I sat down, and turned my attention to Mr. Bradshaw. "Hey, that was a great tip! Do you come here often?"

"No. I only did this time out of curiosity. I have a great many business associates; and as luck would have it, one of them seemed to know what he was talking about today. Don't you agree?"

"It was a very good tip. No, a dynamite tip! What's your line, sir?" I asked.

"Business, investments, trading, buying and selling, when I put my money down I expect a return. I am not a gambler, Mr. Lander. I am the head of Bradshaw Investments International. We invest worldwide. My position as head of this company will be filled by my daughter Connie someday. She is a freshman in college back east."

"So, you are the CEO of a large corporation?"

"No, I am its sole proprietor."

I whistled. "Well, Mr. Bradshaw, may I buy you a drink?"

"Call me Quincy, and I'll buy the drinks. What is your line of work, Mr. Lander?"

"Originally, I was a teacher by profession, computer science at a nearby high school. But the pay was too low and I moved on to other things."

"What things?"

His question made me feel uncomfortable. "I'm between jobs right now. Recently, I operated my own business. I specialized in graphics, web design, and did some occasional networking. But financially, I went in the red and lost it. I had some good months. At other times I couldn't pay the overhead. It was a roller coaster. I'm just not much of a businessman."

"It must take a healthy income to pay for one's time at the track. Do you come here often?"

"No!" I lied. I had tried every racing system in the book, and invented a few of my own. But they work better on paper than in the real world. I wasn't going to tell Quincy this; I wanted his respect.

"You're a personable fellow, Lander, obviously intelligent, with a strong computer background. Have you ever thought of working with a large investment and commodity firm?"

"I never thought of myself as a salesman. Do you mean as a stock broker?"

"No. I mean working as an in-house networking engineer. That's your specialty, right? We really need to upgrade our information processing services. Bradshaw Investments International has worldwide interests. We invest in anything and everything in anticipation of a respectable return in the foreseeable future. I need a specialist to set up and maintain a reliable information base, between numerous work stations. In that respect at the moment, we are rather deficient."

"What kind of investments do you handle, Quincy?"

"I mean real estate, soybean futures, platinum, coffee, bonds and stocks, anything that trades on the open market."

I was impressed. "I see."

"Why don't you come and see me in my office in Corona del Mar on Monday at 10:00 A.M.? Let's talk about this further."

"I've never worked on anything this big, Quincy. It's intimidating."

"Did you have any background in walking before you took your first step, Lander?" Reaching into his pocket, he drew out an expensive looking leather holder from which he pulled out a card, and handed it to me.

"I see what you mean," I replied.

We passed the rest of the afternoon with drinks and conversation. Quincy was an interesting man, a gentleman. I felt comfortable in his presence, and our talk flowed easily from one topic to another. He asked about my family, also telling me about his only child, Connie, whom he had great hopes for. It wasn't until later, that I learned he should have drowned her at birth.

His two companions were engrossed with the races. They frequently walked outside to watch as the horses came over the finish line. I forgot all about playing for the rest of the day. My life had just taken a new turn.

———

I went home that evening. Monica was feeding Linda in the high chair. We lived in a four room apartment in West Covina. She had been a girl's gym teacher at Baldwin Park High School, where I used to teach. When Linda was born, she took a leave of absence to care for her. I had quit during the previous summer break months before. I started up my graphics business with borrowed money. It went belly up after ten months. But I knew I could make it big if I had some cash. I was a horseplayer, and fancied myself as one of that elite one quarter of one per cent of players who could make a living off the track. I went deeper into debt. Sure, I took a beating, but I didn't care. Because I was going to win and pay it all back! I didn't. At least not until later, and not by playing the ponies. Tension was building up between me and Monica. She was on the verge of going back to work, and back to mama.

I walked over to the table as she withdrew the spoon from Linda's mouth. "Monica, look at this!" I spread thirty four one hundred dollar bills on it.

She gasped. "Honey, your system finally worked!"

"No, but I met this guy. He may give me a job. I'm going to see him Monday." We spent the following day, Sunday, having a picnic together. Driving up the road toward Mt. Baldy, we found the perfect spot by the stream. It was one of those balmy, million dollar days one remembers forever. Our marriage was rekindled that day.

Monday, I walked into the stylish building of Bradshaw Investments International and stopped at the security desk blocking my way. "My name is John Lander; I'd like to see Mr. Bradshaw."

"Mr. Lander, take the elevator to the fourth floor. Mr. Bradshaw is expecting you."

Quincy put me right to work. Under the guidance of my new colleagues, I started to dovetail successfully into the organization. He paid me a salary plus bonuses later on, after I started paying my way. I established myself quickly. As my experience grew, I could have gone off on my own, contracting on a larger scale for a multitude of companies. I would have made more money. Such thoughts never occurred to me; I was happy here.

The firm needed a wide area networking system, with constant modifications. I put together a new data base, and installed several servers. This had been my first opportunity to do something this big. Bradshaw was big and I reveled in it. Much of the time I had relatively little to do, except run tests on the hardware and software. I was pretty much my own boss. Sometimes, I didn't have anything to do, but Bradshaw was no sweatshop. Quincy's forte was quality and performance, not time cards. He knew how to choose the very best people. Even Connie inherited her father Quincy's talent for making money. For those good enough to work here, it was like having a second family. Sometimes, Quincy would even pop in and talk to me. He would take various members of his office staff out to lunch on occasion; this often included me.

I saw how they researched global trends, analyzed breaking political situations, anticipated shortages in a market, and watched for leads in the cutting edge of technology. I remember when Enron went down on its knees, and its stock fell below fifty cents a share. Some of the investment specialists were discussing the issue, while I worked nearby on a server. Quincy was there too; he noticed me working in the corner, "What do you think about this Enron situation, Lander?"

"This looks like an opportunity to make some money, Quincy. Enron is the largest pipeline company in America. I think a lot of that loss is pure panic. Maybe I'll put some of my own money into it."

He gave me that easy smile that fit so well on his face. "How big are they Lander? Go for it!"

I did. I bought 10,000 shares for myself at 43 cents per share. The specialists at Bradshaw International ordered another 200,000. It came in real handy later in April of 2005, when it reached over 20 dollars a share. It almost paid for the cost my divorce when Monica left me. I seldom saw him after that. Bradshaw prospered, and so did I, considering I continued to play the horses. Then, Quincy went into semi-retirement. After his daughter, Connie, took over, I never saw him again.

Out on the sidewalk, I detoured away from the parking garage. There was a little place a couple of blocks down the highway where I stopped sometimes to unwind. Two minutes later I walked into bar at the Five Crowns, sat down and ordered my favorite bourbon on the rocks. This was a fun place to have one with the boys after work, but not today. I wanted to be alone, and think things out. I was at the newest crossroads in my life.

I sat there at the bar and looked into my reflection in the whiskey glass. Images from the past flooded my thoughts as I came to grips with who I was. Meet John Lander, thirty-six, two ex-wives, three kids, child support for three kids, and now three ex-careers. I have a fondness for betting the ponies, and a pink slip with three month's severance pay in my pocket. I have a taste for good bourbon; for the graceful lines of a pretty woman; and a fondness for putting everything on the line. Where do I go from here? Guys like me sometimes win big. Why not me?

Two drinks later, my thoughts turned back to Monica. I reached back into my memory to a happy time, remembering when we still dated. How did that go? Yes, I remember it well. It was our first time together in the dimly lit restaurant. The candle was burning on the table as we looked into each other's eyes. "We've been here before," we both said at that same moment. Far fetched, maybe! How can we know something before it happens, or new places or people be familiar? How is déjà vu explained? I have that feeling now, this minute, like something big is going to happen.

As these reflections poured from his memory, he could not realize that destiny would play a wild card into his hand. Fate was knocking at his door. Lander felt himself falling into a trance as he stirred the ice in his glass. Suddenly, he jerked himself back to reality, laid a twenty on the bar and walked out.

4

FOOTSTEPS TO DESTINY

After regaining my strength, I spent less and less time in the medical ward. I began taking long walks on deck. Lost in my own thoughts as I strolled, I remembered those footsteps to destiny that brought me here. I thought of Hank. The Indian Ocean is a great place think over one's mistakes. You know Hank, I reminisced; we weren't so smart after all. We tried to crowd a project into months that required years of work. I groped for answers. Did fate play a hand in this? I remembered vividly that day far in the future when he took me into his confidence.

The doorbell chimed. I glanced up from my Racing Form, shoved it aside and stood up. It rang once more before I opened the door to a Fed-Ex man.

"Package, sir."

"Do I sign for it?"

"No, sir."

"Thank you. Have a good one." Lander took the package.

"You too, sir."

It was a large box. Lander carefully took it to the kitchen table; set it down, and opened it. Inside was the oscilloscope Hank had ordered from Bay View Electronics. Not ordinary, it was a Cadillac in its own right, with industrial capability. It could be networked with Hank's state of the art, dual core Pentium! It would be the key component as a wave control system for the strange device he was building.

Lander had gone into business for himself after being severed from Bradshaw. He had done moderately well. For him, that meant keeping one step ahead of the child support and the bill collectors.

"This is what Hank said he needed," I said out loud. Carefully looking it over, I put it down on the kitchen table, and walked to the phone on the wall. Before I got there, it began ringing. I picked it up and raised it to my ear, "Hello."

It was Monica. "I heard you got fired, Lander; anything to it?"

"My, how things get around, Monica!"

"I still talk to some of the wives of your friends at Bradshaw. Margaret told me. I thought they liked you there."

"It was that creature from hell. The atmosphere at Bradshaw changed when she took over. She never liked me. I think she was planning to get rid of me even before Quincy retired."

"What creature? Who are you talking about?"

"Oh, you remember. You've heard me talk about her before, the change in management, Quincy Bradshaw's daughter. But

I know you have more on your mind than my welfare, Monica. What's up?"

"How about the child support, John? You didn't forget; did you?"

"In the mail today, never you fear. Just a temporary cash flow problem. I'm getting paid for a job today."

"What are you going to do with yourself? Are you hanging around the track now?"

"Monica, don't let it worry your pretty head; you've got no claim on me anymore."

"John, you don't have to take that attitude with me. I was just concerned, that's all. We can still be friends."

"How are Linda and Tracy?"

"In need of an attentive father, take a hint? They ask about you all the time."

"I know; I know, but I've been real busy. I'm working on something right now."

"Handicapping takes a lot of brainwork, John Lander. Give it up; get a job! You know you have a gambling problem; don't you? Why don't you get some counseling?"

"How I spend my time right now is none of your business, Monica! When we were still together, you and the girls never went without. Did you?"

"Don't flatter yourself!"

"I don't want to talk about it any more. I heard you were getting married."

"Maybe! I'm pretty sure. He's a nice guy, makes good money and is kind to the girls."

"I didn't hear you say that little word love. Where is it?"

"A girl can love a rich, stable guy just as quick as a wild card, Lander; and the ride can be a little smoother. Life with you was a roller coaster. It was fun for a while, but a girl can only take so much before she has to get off."

"What does he do again; doctor?"

"Radiologist."

"Look, Monica; I'm real busy now. Can we chitchat another time?"

"OK, but call the girls. They still need their dad too. Bye!"

"I will. Bye yourself, Monica!"

He looked at the phone in his hand before hanging it up. What kind of father am I? At least Linda and Tracy know me. How about my son, Andrew? Since my first divorce I've seen him only a half dozen times in thirteen years. His mother moved to Florida. She met some guy there and married rich. I wonder if he ever thinks about his dad. Well, three more years and his child support is history.

I walked into my office, sat down at my desk and reached for the checkbook. I wrote one for Andrew's next child support payment; then I placed it in an envelope and addressed it to Teresa Walters in Fort Myers Beach, Florida. I did the same for Monica. Both would go out this morning. I put them in my coat pocket and walked back to the kitchen.

I stood there for a second staring at the oscilloscope. Then I remembered; I was going to call Hank. I turned and walked to the phone, picked it up and dialed.

"Hello," he answered.

"It's here, Hank. I think this is what you need, but will have to work out the details later when I see you."

"When can you start, John? Everything depends on that piece of equipment."

"I can come over by ten o'clock. I'll leave here in fifteen minutes. I'm just going to stop at the post office first."

"I'll be waiting."

"Oh, Hank; can you pay in cash today? It would save me a move."

"Well, I suppose I can go to the bank if I have to. You won't take a check?"

"I've got a tight schedule. I really would appreciate it."

"OK, I'll have it here waiting for you. That was seven hundred and fifty dollars; right?"

"That's right, Hank. You already paid for the oscilloscope, so seven fifty finishes the job. Goodbye; see you at ten."

"Until then, John!"

Funny about old Hank. He's one of the few guys that still call me John. But he has ever since I was in his class at Cal Poly. If I can zip through this job by noon, I can be at Del Mar by first post.

Irritating, Hank thought. He wants cash. Why can't he take a check like everybody else? Oh well, I can be back in twenty minutes.

Henry Martin, or Hank as everyone called him, had retired years before from Cal Poly. He had been a physics professor there, earning top honors. He had even worked on hush hush defense projects at Livermore when he was a young man. His home was in an upscale but older area of Laguna Hills. His wife Jennifer had become estranged in the late 1980s, when she left him for a younger man. She took their investments as her share of their estate, and Hank kept the house. This was most important to him; he needed the workshop. His research was all he lived for.

His workshop was a large prefab steel building behind the house. Normal entrance could only be gained through a locked steel door connected by an overhang to his house. This had always been a source of irritation to Jennifer. She thought it was ugly, and couldn't understand why he needed so much secrecy. He lied to her about its purpose, telling her he needed to protect his research in magnetic levitation. Having no interest in science, Jennifer stayed out of his way. She seldom saw the inside.

Hank returned from the bank and walked into his study where he sat down in his favorite chair. He picked up his favorite book from the end table, and carefully opened it. This was Einstein's work on his unified field theory, the one that was never finished. Einstein's equations suggested the possibility of time travel. This had fascinated Hank since he was in high school. It only intensified after he graduated with a master's degree in physics and received his teacher's credential. As time passed, he advanced further earning his doctorate and becoming a major player in his field.

The words on the paper bounced around in his consciousness as they had so many times before. Hank laid the book on his lap, and closed his eyes. How many times had these same thoughts haunted him? Space-time curves. And if the universe rotates, like the best minds among scientists and mathematicians believe, the possibility of time travel may be a reality, even commonplace. How many of Einstein's equations had already been solved which yielded time travel solutions? Was it in the hundreds?

This concept was known as the Einstein-Rosen Bridge, wormholes into other dimensions. Out of this grew the theory of the black hole. Later, the idea was expanded to include the spinning wormhole. This spinning wormhole interested Hank above all else. Anyone entering one of these would theoretically emerge into another dimension of time and space. Did these funnel-like bridges really connect different continuums of space and time? Hank believed he had the answer.

Shadows of this went back to the infamous alleged experiment on the USS Eldridge in WWII. American scientists supposedly used this principle to make this ship disappear. Or did they? Allegedly, large generators were used to produce counter-rotating energy fields. This created a negative energy, opening up an Einstein-Rosen bridge. As the story goes, this caused the ship to be projected into the future briefly, but produced hazardous consequences to the crew from radiation and from the co-mingling of matter. But if this was true, what went wrong? The men were unshielded from radiation! This was as bad as swimming with crocodiles. The story about the Eldridge was later debunked, but not totally. If Hank had learned anything in the last quarter of the 20th century, it was that the government would lie. Then, follow up the lie with unlimited cover-ups. One thing was certain; both Einstein and Tesla had worked secretly for the U.S. Government during the war.

Now, he would have the oscilloscope. After two years of trial and error, the space-time device could be completed. The oscilloscope was the key to controlling the device. With it, Hank could read the strength of these energy fields and regulate the desired wavelength. This was crucial. The multi-trillions of combinations produced by these fields determined where one could go within the vortex of the energy field. Ordinary control and modulation systems would not work. This required fine tuning to the ultimate degree.

Lander was essential to making this work. Hank could not network the oscilloscope between the Pentium and magnetic polarization box. The upper limits of computer hardware were beyond his training. He had been Lander's physics instructor at Cal Poly. They met years later when both took computer graphics classes together in the early '90s. They renewed their acquaintance, even becoming friends. Once, Lander solved a real sticky hardware problem for him. After that, Hank hired him exclusively to solve his computer issues.

The doorbell rang; Hank answered the door. "John, come in."

"I hope this works for you, Hank. How are your experiments in magnetic levitation going?"

This was an uncomfortable question. Magnetic levitation was his standard lie to anyone who had seen his machine. "As well as can be expected, John. Let's get started right away!" He led Lander to the rear of his house and through the breezeway to his workshop. Unlocking its door, Hank walked in and flipped on the light switch, followed by Lander. He locked the door behind them. His two powerful Alturdyne generators placed side by side came into view. Years before, Hank managed to buy them used at a good price. The two men walked past them, through the middle of the shop which was cluttered with machine tools toward the far side.

Here it was. Hank just called it the Machine. It was an eight foot high vertical cylinder, covered with lead sheets, and was surrounded by a framework which housed alternate layers of magnetic inductors. A lead sheathed door occupied a niche on the side. Several feet to the right was the control center. From this station, what seemed like a myriad of wires connected the computer, its monitor and accessories to the magnetic polarization box adjoining the machine. This box had been the heart of this project. It was Hank's own creation. It contained a matrix of smetic-A liquid crystals which polarized the magnetic waves coming from both generators, allowing the positive currents from each to flow through one another. This created the negative energy required to open the vortex of a spinning wormhole.

Initially, he realized there was a major problem with the concept of time travel. Hank was concerned with reconciling the problem of the duplication of atoms. How does one take atoms back to a prior time, where those same atoms already exist? This would prove to be unfounded, merely a mental hurdle. It was a matter of over-thinking the issue. Again, those wonderful geniuses of physics solved this with their discovery of multitudes of particles. Some of which only fleetingly appeared, then were gone. These phantom particles were mirror images of their counterparts in this world, yet they rapidly disappeared into another space-time continuum. Where did they go? Into any time/space dimension allowing for the possibility of an unending stream of identical or near identical universes.

Lander set about networking the oscilloscope into the linkage between the magnetic polarization box and the computer. It wasn't easy. This was virgin ground he was breaking. It had to be learned as he went along. Six hours later he was still at it and growing irritated. "I have some issues with this Hank. I may have to think about it and try to finish the job tomorrow." He wasn't trying to escape to the track; that was already a lost cause. This was not an easy project.

"I'm really anxious for you to finish this, John."

"OK, but I'm going to take a break. I'll get something to eat, and work late if you want. But I'll have to charge you a little more money."

"This means a lot to me, John. Of course."

"What if I come back at six? Does that work for you?

"John, it's a quarter after four now, let's break. See you at six."

Lander left and Hank went inside his house. He sat down and closed his eyes to rest. He remembered back six months earlier. It was then he had placed an ordinary crescent wrench into the chamber where the vortex of his opposing magnetic fields would be created. Retiring to his shielded control station, he had applied minimum power in a short burst. After shutting it down, he checked the inside of the chamber. No change! Finally, after numerous tries with longer and greater durations of power, he felt a muted vibration throughout the workshop. Something was happening! Hank remembered scouring the chamber for any trace of the wrench. None at all! Where had it gone? This must be the Einstein-Rosen Bridge he was looking for. The crescent wrench was gone forever.

Hank relived that moment over and over in his mind every day of these last six months. But there was a problem. He hadn't been able to duplicate the event. Monitoring and fine-tuning this equipment wasn't possible without the oscilloscope. It was also apparent that this was a two man job. Someone must remain in the lab to work the controls. Whoever passed through the bridge was at the mercy of the controlling end. He could not accomplish this alone. Lander, what about Lander? Do I dare bring him into my plan?

———

It was late evening before Lander finished. "I don't see how this machine of yours could magnetically levitate anything."

"Do you remember studying magnetism, John?"

"Yes, but I never saw anything like this."

"Suppose you're right; why don't we go into my study and have a drink?"

"I don't have to be asked twice."

Hank pulled down his event log from the shelf above his workstation and tucked it under his arm. In it, he had kept meticulous records, carefully cataloguing every detail and event connected to the device. They both went into the study. "What'll you have, John?"

"I'm partial to bourbon."

"I think I have something you'll like." Hank pulled a bottle of Gentleman Jack and two glasses out of a liquor cabinet. He placed them on the small table between two reclining chairs at right angles to each other. This had been his and Jennifer's favorite spot when they were still together. "Sit down. I'll get us some ice." Hank returned from the kitchen, placed a small bucket of ice between them, then sat down and motioned for me to help myself.

He waited until I took a sip and then began his story. "John, this project is colossal, groundbreaking and controversial. It's too big for me and I don't know where it's going to end. How do I best explain this to you? I need a confidant who can work with me. What's your main interest in life, John?"

"I want lots and lots of money, and women."

"Well, at least you're honest about it. What do you care about science, power or politics?"

"I don't," I replied.

"John, you seem to be happy with a world that I would like to leave behind."

"It's the only one I know."

"I don't have anyone anymore. Jennifer and I were childless. My work is all I have. I long for a better place, and I have a special one in mind."

"Ha, ha, ha! Are you going to magnetically levitate yourself out of this world, Hank?"

The professor was pensive, almost somber until finally speaking. "Maybe! In a manner of speaking, John. Did you ever consider that perhaps time is not linear as we are led to believe? But maybe it's more like a vibrating guitar string; where the past, present and future are always there, blending together in the cosmos beyond anything we can understand. How can anyone explain the marvels of Nostradamus, or of Edgar Cayce? How do these special people see into the past or future unless it's always there?"

"I don't know," I replied. But the professor had gained my interest.

"Do you know who Edgar Cayce was?"

"I've heard the name," I replied. "Didn't he have something to do with the paranormal?"

"Yes, that's right. Cayce gave over 14,000 readings. He helped people find cures to their illnesses. He explained mysteries of the past, and gave accurate predictions of the future. How could he do that, unless somehow all of these are interconnected beyond our understanding? Cayce's exact words were, 'Time is an illusion that has purpose.' What do you think of that?"

"Wow," was all I could say.

Seeing my drink was gone, Hank told me to help myself as he explained his project. I listened, fascinated, riveted to his story. The alcohol failed to dim my mind as my attention soaked up his every word. "So you see, it was not a dream; the crescent wrench disappeared from the chamber. It had to go someplace. In order to follow through, I need someone I can trust, someone who is not motivated by lust for power, fame or who will betray my work. No one other than me must ever know about this device except a trustworthy colleague. No government can ever have this, John. It dies with me."

"Professor Martin, how do I fit in to your plans?" I asked with deep respect.

"I need someone who can continuously help me calibrate this machine. This person will be my confidant. One of us must control this device from this end; the other must go through. You are the best computer networking engineer I know, and you have three qualities that recommend you for the job."

I reverted back to our familiar style. "What are those, Hank?"

"To begin with, all you want is money. Second, you're not some flaming activist who wants to rewrite history; you don't want power over other people. Third, you are a much younger man. I'm sixty-eight. What might lie in wait out there, could easily overtax my physical ability. As for me, all I want is to escape to a better time, far into the future where mankind has ironed out all of its ills. I'm a lonely man. I don't belong here; I feel like I never did!"

"Tell me more, Hank."

"We work as a team, John. We can use the Einstein-Rosen Bridge to our mutual advantage. I think I know a way to enrich you in the process of completing my quest for a new home."

"How, professor?"

"We'll send probes into the future, checking out the various eras until I discover where I want to be. Along the way we'll watch for financial opportunities, especially in the near future, for you to invest in."

Visions of knowing advance track and lottery results tantalized me.

"You should have plenty of opportunities to enrich yourself before you catapult me into the future. What do you think about that?"

"I'm your man!" I said with a smile.

Before we parted that night, he handed me his ledger; "Guard it carefully, and read it. You have to catch up with me. The only thing you won't learn about is the magnetic polarization box. It is the key to this project and I won't share its secret with anyone."

chapter

5

THE MACHINE

I was growing restless. The Brits were nice to us but I was getting anxious to get off this cruiser. Only fourteen more hours of sailing time remained to Darwin. It was time for mess so I headed for the galley. As I slowly ate my supper, I began thinking about the machine Hank created. Then I smiled, suddenly remembering; it won't be created until sixty years from now. You know, Hank; this is ironic. We never were in charge; the machine controlled us. We were only pawns in a bigger game. Remember, John Lander; remember the machine?

Over the next several weeks we experimented heavily with various frequencies. We were able to tap into untold millions of combinations of possible destinations through the vortex.

Weeks became months. The work progressed, but our confidence scarcely grew, having sent out over 3,000 probes. Early on, all of them were lost. They could have landed anywhere, some primeval sea maybe; who knows! Then we hit pay dirt from one wavelength; forty-four probes were sent, forty-four returned. The last of these probes sent was a modified camcorder. Then, we brought it back. It contained images and sounds revealing the presence of orange trees, and familiar animals! We recognized mockingbirds, sparrows, doves and quail. Whether the probe had gone backward or forward, we didn't know. Then Hank decided to send the parakeets through. He did within the next half hour, and then we brought them back. They were fine, and had been shielded perfectly. Detecting no residual radiation in the chamber, we repeated this test several times. I fine tuned the settings.

It was crucial that the vortex remain at least partially closed when not needed. It wouldn't be very practical to leave the vortex permanently open in recall configuration. Anyone or anything could accidentally step into it and enter our time. Displacing animals could be serious enough; displacements of people would be disastrous. Of equal importance, we couldn't career off into some other space-time without being certain of coming back. One of us would always have to be at the control station. The same wavelength would have to be carefully monitored to allow safe passage through the bridge.

Recall was a problem that had to be worked out too. We needed a way to modify the opening of the vortex to allow for passage of a signal. I suggested that we try lowering the power level so that only electro-magnetic waves could pass through, and not heavy matter. We needed to test this concept. Hank and

I made a small transmitter. We sent it through and then lowered the power level. It worked. At low levels of power, the vortex partially opened up. The transmission signal returned through the vortex. We now had a way to signal without leaving the bridge all the way open. A recall signal sent from the small transmitter at the opposite end, would alert the operator left behind when to trigger an increase in power. This would allow for the return flow of heavy matter from the opposite dimension, and back into the chamber of the machine. We repeated this test several times over the next few days. So far things were working out pretty well. Hank recorded all of this in his event log. Everything had to be precise.

I frequently stayed at Hank's house. We worked from first light until well after midnight. These days passed by so fast for me; I was hardly aware of the hours. Exhaustion began taking hold, and one evening I decided to pull the plug on the project early. I told Hank I'd see him the next day and went home for the night. Totally forgetting about supper, I poured myself a double shot of bourbon over ice and carried it with me as I made my way up to my bedroom. I gulped it down and allowed myself to collapse on my bed fully clothed, where I quickly drifted into a deep sleep.

Vaguely feeling light and warmth dancing on my eyelids, I slowly roused. One glance at the clock told me I had slept a solid eight hours. It was mid-morning as I rose out of bed, making my way to the shower. An hour later, I was sipping coffee in the kitchen. I called Hank. He was already at work in

the laboratory. I told him I wouldn't be in until late afternoon.
I had to have more money soon. My severance pay was long
gone. And, I wasn't bringing in any from side jobs. I had been
drawing cash off my credit cards and they were about to burst.
As my share of our divorce settlement, I was allowed to keep
the house. Monica had received all of our liquid assets. The
house wasn't paid for and I had a large payment. But I did have
considerable equity in it. I would take out a second loan on the
house. But how could I get a loan approved without being able
to show an income. I wasn't ready to sell my place. It was the
only material thing I had to show for my life's work. I didn't
want any unnecessary questions either.

One of the bonuses of working at Bradshaw for all those
years, was that I met a lot of people in the world of finance. I
retrieved my business card file from my desk; sat down by the
phone as I thumbed through the Rolodex until I found what
I wanted. I stopped when I reached the name, Tim Cramer,
Washington Mutual. We had become pals in the bar at the Five
Crowns. Tim had some past dealings with Quincy, and had
even tried to get me to play golf with him on several occasions.
Now, I wished I had taken him up on it. He also told me that
he was good at fixing up real estate loans. Well, I would soon
find out if I still had any calling cards with him. I dialed his
business number.

The phone rang at the offices of Washington Mutual. A
young woman answered. "Washington Mutual, may I help you?"

"Yes, mam. Is Mr. Cramer available?"

"Who should I say is calling please?"

"John Lander."

"Please hold while I check."

Within seconds a man's voice came on the line. "Lander, how the hell are you? I haven't seen you since forever."

"I haven't been around since twice that long, Tim. How are things with you?"

"Just trying to make enough money to keep up with the old lady's wish list. How are things at Bradshaw?"

"I don't work there any longer."

"I thought you liked it there, Lander."

"It wasn't exactly my choice, but it's probably for the best."

"Tough break, huh! Are you looking to borrow some money on your house?"

"You guessed it, Tim; you're pretty good!"

"It's my business, Lander; I eat and breathe this stuff. How about meeting me for lunch in about an hour?"

"I thought you'd never ask. Where at?"

"The Place Across The Street from the Hotel Laguna."

"We might have a long wait getting a table there at noon, Tim. That's a popular place and it's always tourist season in Laguna!"

"Maybe not, they know me well. And it doesn't matter if we do wait. I don't punch a time clock, buddy."

"Until then, Tim!"

"Till then, Lander!"

An hour and a half later, we were sitting across from each other in the restaurant. It was packed with tourists as usual. A pretty waitress in a short skirt came over to us. "What can I get for you boys to drink?"

"Budweiser," Tim said.

"Budweiser," she repeated.

"Bring me a girlfriend in a green dress," I said.

She giggled.

"That sounds good, you better bring me one of those too!" said Tim.

The cute waitress was bubbly. She went along with the joke. "OK, a girlfriend in a green dress. And that is?"

"A Heineken," I replied.

"A Heinie!" She giggled again and hustled off to the bar.

"I thought you were a bourbon on the rocks type guy?" asked Tim.

"Too early in the day, I want to keep a clear head."

"Wow, this must be serious. You know, Lander; why don't you leave that computer geek type crap behind. I can get you a position with my company and you can learn what it's like to make some real money."

"Penguins don't fly, Tim. I am what I am."

He looked at me like I was some kind of a dumb S.O.B; but I could tell that he was trying to be my friend. "What gives, Lander? What do you need?"

The waitress showed up just then with two bottles of beer and two glasses. She put them down, grabbed her pad and took a pencil from behind her ear. "Have you boys decided what you want?"

"Just a club sandwich for me, hun," Tim said.

"I'll have the same please," I echoed.

"OK boys, two club sandwiches!" She quickly scribbled the order. We both fell silent as we mutually admired her posterior as she headed toward the kitchen.

I turned my attention back to Tim. "When I got the sack at Bradshaw, I struck out on my own. Now, I've become involved in a special project. I have been working on it for months, full time; and frankly, I can think of little else."

I could see he was only mildly interested. "What project, Lander?"

"Can't talk about it, a big secret! I might want to patent it," I lied.

"And you need a second mortgage, right, I understand. But you can get a loan all over town. Processing you through will be easy."

"There's a catch, Tim. I can't show any income right now; I don't have an employer. Also, I can't let anyone know what I'm working on."

"That good, huh! Now you got me wondering what you're up to." His interest visibly increased. "Well, that's not hard to fix. A lot of people owe me favors. I think we can get the books cooked. And I'll see that you get the maximum loan on the appraisal."

"Thanks, Tim!" We went on to discuss my departure from Bradshaw, and I told him the story about Connie Randall firing me. Before long my bottle was empty. Luckily the waitress showed up just then with our sandwiches. I held up the empty bottle for her to see. "Sweetie, my girlfriend left me, and all I have to show for it is her empty green dress. Would you see if you can find her twin?"

"Another girlfriend, OK; keep that Heinie coming. And how about you, sweetie?" she asked, looking at Tim.

"Oh yes, don't forget me."

Suddenly, Tim looked hard at me. "You know, Lander; I see Quincy on the golf course once in a while. Why don't I put in a word for you?"

"No, Tim. This was the push I needed for a long time. My mind is like a train on the track. I can only go in one direction, think of one thing right now. If you say anything to Quincy at all, just say that you saw me and I'm doing well. Please?"

"Sure, Lander; whatever you say."

We spent two hours over lunch, and I was beginning to enjoy myself too much. Five girlfriends later I had a good glow and a mild buzz. When we left the restaurant, He told me to swing by his office and we would get the application going. Well, I thought; it's probably no fun taking care of business with a clear head anyway. I told him I would, and we went to our separate cars in the parking lot.

———

Our preliminary work was completed. Now it was my turn. Hank was too old. When it was his turn to go, we had to have all of the details worked out. I fastened the return beacon to my belt. Hank sat at the control station. He would automatically bring me back from that location two minutes later in case the beacon didn't work. If there was a problem, I would need to get out of there fast. I closed myself into the chamber, and took a position within the core of the vortex. Soon, the high pitched electrical current started whizzing about my head. I realized I should have brought ear muffs. I felt as if I were weightless and falling within a dark funnel. At this, the moment of truth, I was horrified, wishing I had never become part of this project.

Then I touched dirt and fell backwards, landing first on my butt, then sprawling on my back. I had passed through and into the orange grove. Looking up between the branches I saw a few sparse clouds, and heard aircraft engines, definitely the sound of propellers! Bees were buzzing about the trees. Relieved now that

I was safe, I saw humor in my situation. A rather inglorious way to arrive for someone who has traveled so far to be here! But, what the hell, this isn't so bad. When I first came into the light in my own world, I was bloody and naked to boot. I repositioned myself and brushed away the dirt on my coveralls. After the two minute interval, I passed back through. This time I told Hank to set the machine for an automatic return at twenty minute intervals, and maintain the bridge open for thirty seconds each time. That would give me a chance to look around. As long as I was in the vortex at any of those times, I would return even if my beacon failed to signal recall.

I hesitated. "Do you have a pistol in the house, Hank?"

"Yes, what's the matter?" He looked concerned. "Did you see anything to give you cause for alarm?"

"Just a precaution, if things go bad, I might not get another chance. And, I need some hearing protection too."

"Wait here, John; I'll be right back."

I waited there several minutes while he went inside his house. Going to his bedroom, Hank took his PPK from a drawer in the nightstand, also taking out an extra loaded clip. He pulled down a set of ear muffs from his closet shelf. Returning to the workshop, he handed these to me. The PPK fit neatly into my right coveralls pocket, and I placed the extra magazine in the left one. We rechecked the settings and finalized them. I shut myself into the chamber, and again was passed through.

Knowing what to expect, I landed on my feet this time. I walked toward the edge of the orchard, about eighty feet away. The soft soil was sliding over the tops of my shoes and around my socks. I broke into the clear where a dirt road passed by the grove. I saw a wood framed farmhouse to my right maybe an eighth mile away and another to my left even farther. I walked toward the closer house. Approaching, I turned onto the dirt drive and noticed the name Woodward on the mailbox. I could see an antique John Deere tractor in front of a barn. Sounds coming from a multitude of birds could be heard in the chicken house behind the barn. Wherever I was in time, I hadn't gone very far.

I walked up the drive to the house and knocked on the door. An old man who looked to be in his mid-60s in faded overalls came to the door. "Howdy, what brings you out this way?" he asked.

"Hello, sir. My car broke down. I'm lost. Could you give me some directions?"

"Sure, come on in young feller and have a glass of iced tea." He was more friendly and at ease than I would have expected from a stranger. He yelled to his wife. "Rosemary, pour a glass of iced tea for the stranger here."

Looking around the living room I saw maple furniture, and on a wall in the adjoining kitchen, a hand cranked phone. I was in the past.

"What brings you out this way, mister?"

"I was driving these back country roads for pleasure and broke down. I didn't bring a map. And then I started walking. I wasn't paying attention to signs. What town are we close to, sir?"

"You're not far off Topanga Canyon Road, a couple of miles from Chatsworth. Just go down to the crossroads and turn right. There's a gas station about a mile yonder, and they have a tow truck. You can call them from here."

His wife handed me the tea. "I hope you enjoy this, sir; it's fresh brewed."

I took a deep swallow. It was cool and sweet. "Thank you, mam." I looked back at Mr. Woodward. "Do you have a calendar I could look at, sir?"

"Sure, come on in the kitchen." He pointed me to the calendar on the wall while he walked to the phone. "I'll call Charlie down at the station and we'll get you fixed up."

"Sir, please don't call him yet. I was enjoying walking, and I would rather go there on foot."

He looked at me skeptically. "Well, if that's what you want to do!"

"You see, I work long hours inside an office, and really appreciate a chance to walk. This is a real treat for me." I faced the calendar. 1945! From the marks on it I could see this was springtime. "Sir, what is the exact date?"

"May 11, young feller. I would've figured anyone working in an office would know that," he said in an offhand but still friendly manner. "And I would think his boss would make him get a haircut too."

"I've had a few days off sir, just relaxing. I wanted to get away and be alone." I filed the haircut remark in my memory.

Woodward nodded his head. "I can understand that, with the war and all. What do you do anyway?"

"Defense research, but I can't talk about it." I hoped this line would get me off the hook from answering more questions.

He nodded. The old gentleman wanted to talk more about the war. He had grandsons in the service. I listened respectfully as I drank down the iced tea. Then I thanked the old couple and looked at my watch. "I have to go now."

The old gentleman looked at my watch. "Fancy watch, I ain't never seen one like that before."

I smiled. "You can believe there will be many more like it someday."

"And I never seen shoes like them, neither."

The alarm bells went off in my head. I was wearing a pair of Reeboks. If I was going to dance through time, I would have to become less conspicuous. If this old farmer could pick up these details, what would a serious observer or a policeman notice? "Oh, they are a new fancy import, nothing to brag about really."

I turned down the road in the direction he had pointed. I started walking away from the house, only turning to wave good-bye. A little further along, I glanced back over my shoulder. He was walking around his house toward the barn. When he was out of sight, I ducked into the orange grove and plodded back to my entry point. It took me what seemed like a long time to find my arrival spot. Over an hour had gone by since I had passed through the bridge. Locating it, I waited patiently for the next sixteen minutes to go by in order to complete the twenty minute recall interval. Seconds before the anticipated moment, I positioned my ear muffs. I quickly felt the vibration and muted noise of the vortex, and passed back through. I opened the door of the chamber and stood there grinning. Hank got up from the work station and hurried over to me. In awe, he stood there eagerly waiting for me to speak.

"1945, Hank! What an opportunity!"

Hank carefully recorded all of the details in his event log as I shut the machine down. Shortly, he turned off the lights at the workshop entrance as we walked out. He closed and locked the door. We went into his study and headed straight for his small bar. He took out a half empty bottle of Gentleman Jack and two empty glasses, placing them between us as we stood there. We forgot all about ice. This was a crowning moment for both of us. I poured a long stiff drink. Downing most of it in one gulp, I refilled my glass before plopping in a chair.

"1945! Do you realize what we can do with this?"

He looked disappointed. "That's not the right direction, John."

"Look, Hank; I have an idea. We need money to continue, right? Do you need money?"

"Yes, John, I have a whopping unpaid electric bill of $4,000. The machine eats a lot of electric power."

"I go back in time, Hank, and make a few well placed bets. You see what I'm getting at? I'll collect some big bucks and come back. Then we'll have all the money we need. You'll be able to finish your project."

"I'm scared. We might accidentally alter the past. We don't know what we're doing."

"Hank, we can clean up. It's our chance to put the equipment to the test. I can go back, spend a few weeks there and set us up forever. For you, time will only amount to a few seconds. You advance the settings to pick me back up from there five or six weeks later. I say let's go for it."

"I don't know, John; I need to think. Can we talk about this tomorrow? I'm tired. I want to sleep on this."

"OK, I'll go home. Call me in the morning. You know there has to be some risk. You knew that when you started, right?" He nodded. I downed my drink and left for home.

Hank filled his glass half full before he allowed his head to collapse backward against the head rest of his easy chair. Slowly his thoughts went back to high school. The memory was still fresh in his mind after all these years, those few minutes that would define his future. It was in the last days of the Korean War. Luckily, I was too young for the war. I didn't line up age wise for Vietnam either. I remember as if it were yesterday. There I was again, waiting outside the principal's office with a black eye. The principal had just finished talking to the boy who gave it to me, Jimmie Lee Smith. Jimmie looked pretty bad himself as he walked out of the principal's office. He scowled at me as he passed by.

"Come in here, Henry," Mr. Wilson said sternly. "Sit down. Fighting over what, Henry? What do you have to say for yourself?"

"We weren't fighting exactly, Mr. Wilson. We were just scuffling. And Jimmie got sore, that's all."

Mr. Wilson cut me off. "You know that's against the rules. You are truant all the time, and have been caught smoking on campus. How many times have you been in my office this semester? How many fights, Henry? You don't seem to relate very well to other people. You're a loner. Where will it end, Henry Martin?"

Then came a knock on the door. "Yes, come in," answered Mr. Wilson.

Mr. Hawks, my math and science teacher stepped inside. "Mr. Wilson, would it be alright to have a word with Henry after you've finished with him?"

"Of course it will, if you think he'll listen."

"Henry, please stop and see me in the outer office before you go home?"

I nodded. He left the room and Mr. Wilson chided me some more. My punishment was cumulative. I was given two weeks suspension for all of my past sins. Dad would be ever so mad; he was strictly a straight shooter. I walked out of Mr. Wilson's office and up to Mr. Hawks without saying anything, and just stood there in front of him.

"Henry, you are selling yourself short in life. You are getting through my class now with a low C and you don't even study. There are better things for you out there. But you are going to flunk if you don't come around. There's plenty of room at the bottom in life, and you don't have to stand in line to get there."

"What do you mean, Mr. Hawks?"

"Just this, Henry; you have too much mentality to waste yourself like this. I know your dad; you come from a good family. He is a friend of mine and he is in my blue lodge. What did Mr. Wilson do to you?"

"Two weeks suspension," I replied.

"OK, Henry, I'll do this much for you. You're suspended during school hours only. You show up in my classroom at 3:45 and I'll personally tutor you."

"Why would you do that, Mr. Hawks?"

"Because you're not a throw-away. What's most important in this life needs to be passed on. Each generation owes that much to the next one, which must fill their shoes someday."

I realized this man cared what would become of me. He was willing to give up his time; and anyway, I didn't want to repeat the school year. "OK, Mr. Hawks! When do we start?"

"Tomorrow, Hank. Why don't I just call you Hank? Come at three forty-five like I said."

From then on Mr. Hawks captured my imagination, until I absorbed his wonderful philosophy. He taught me that mathematics is the language of God. And everything could be described with numbers if you learned his language. I also learned from him that physics were the rules by which God governed the universe. He not only brought me up to date with my class but introduced me to the ideas of Archimedes, Newton, Tesla, Einstein and a host of others. I became a devotee of these great pioneers, especially of Einstein.

I finished Mr. Hawks' classes with an A. I also brought up my other grades. My parents were visibly pleased with the change in me. I carried this enthusiasm into college with resolve, and followed through by getting my degree in physics with a teaching certificate. I devoured every bit of information I could find on the subject of time travel. And everything came back to this, the Einstein-Rosen Bridge.

In 1986, I was still teaching physics at Cal Poly. I had met Jennifer back in graduate school in 1959. We got married shortly after I received my master's degree. My world was centered on research. Jennifer wanted material things along with an active social life. Not that my salary wasn't good, but we had no children. Jennifer had too much time on her hands. She met a younger man one Saturday afternoon; that was when our marriage of twenty-five years ended.

When did I first meet John Lander? As I recall, he signed up for one of my physics classes. What was it that he wanted to do? I really don't quite remember. Somewhere along the line he shifted to computers. Well, that seems to be the wave of the future. He was a good student when he could shift his keep off girls. Then, I met him years later. We were both taking some computer graphics courses. We always had coffee together during breaks. And then he solved a nagging hardware problem in my PC. John was good at it. Even after going to work for Bradshaw he still had time to help me.

Hank's mind began going numb. Did any of this really happen? He wondered. Exhausted, sleep unexpectedly overwhelmed him.

Miles away, I walked into my living room as my mind was racing. I couldn't think of anything except for that last conversation with Hank. I placed a handful of mail on the kitchen table, sat down, and began looking through it. The escrow instructions were there. I had to unwind before I opened the envelope. I got back up, walked over and poured myself a stiff shot of bourbon. Returning to the table, I sat back down and pulled the papers from the envelope. After signing them in a multitude of locations, I placed everything into the large envelope that came with them. No, I thought; I won't mail them. I'll deliver them myself tomorrow morning.

Visions of my past began to flood my conscience. My thoughts turned back to Monica. We grew further apart during those last four years we were together. She was materialistic one way and I was obsessed in others. Horseracing had been an ongoing passion of mine. I was always looking for a 'get rich quick scheme.' Not a real good backdrop for our marriage.

My adult life continued to pass in front of me as I poured and consumed my second drink. I thought back to Teresa. We met at Cal Poly in my senior year. I think it was in Hank's class. I was studying electrical engineering in those days. Then I became fascinated with computers. From then on, I knew what I wanted to do, and switched my major to computer science. Teresa and I married after I graduated. She came from a well to do family, and was more materialistic than I could provide for on a novice teacher's salary. We had few interests in common outside of the bedroom and kitchen. She left me after only two years and took our son Andrew away. Then I met Monica at the high school. She was the girl's gym teacher. She had stunning good looks and short dark hair. We dated steadily. After we married, I upgraded my education by studying computer graphics at night. Soon, I was able to make extra money building web sites on the side. This became secondary, as I honed my networking skills. The computer industry was constantly changing. One either stayed on the technical cusp or became an 'also ran.'

One Saturday, two of my teacher colleagues invited me to spend the afternoon with them at Santa Anita. I won eight hundred dollars that day, and it had seemed 'oh so easy.' On weekends I became a regular at the track. My luck held for what seemed a long time. I knew I was going to make it big. My plans included working for myself and playing the horses.

That first summer after Monica and I married, I started up my business. I also developed system upon system of betting the ponies. And then my luck went south permanently. The business failed and my marriage with Monica almost did too. In 1997 I met Quincy, and my life turned around. After another strong drink, I walked to my bedroom. "1945," I muttered, "I look forward to this adventure."

Next morning, I delivered the signed copies of the escrow instructions. Tim was pretty smart. He knew his profession. A scant three weeks had passed before I was signing the final papers in front of the notary at the escrow office. The loan funded that very day and I was able to pick up my check later that afternoon. This worked out well for me.

———

Hank and I resolved our ideas about venturing into 1945. I convinced him that this would indeed set us up for a run into the future.

"I'll leave this cesspool of the post-twentieth century behind, John. Out there, somewhere to come, mankind will have learned to live with itself. I've always believed in that Utopia. I'm going to find it. Maybe they can even knock a few years off my age. When the time comes, John, after I'm gone, it will be your responsibility to destroy the machine." Hank repeated this to me so many times during these days.

I was skeptical. "I've already promised you that. But what if you don't like it there?"

"We'll know that, after we do some exploring."

"Sure, Hank!"

"You can't just go cold turkey into 1945, John. We need money from that era, and in large quantities. It's easy enough to get silver dollars, but most of the paper money printed then has been destroyed. In the quantities we need, it can be rare and expensive."

"I've already taken out a second mortgage, Hank. I had to. These last few months I have run my credit cards up to their limits. Now I have money to work with."

"I'll do the same, John; we'll go in half and half. We need a lot of paper money, and none of it can be printed after 1945.

Some of the money you take back, you'll have to use to live on while you're there. That's an expense of doing business; we can't help it, and we'll just share that cost. Whatever we net from your recovery will be our joint reward after we deduct the cost of maintaining the machine. Does that seem fair to you?"

"That sounds good to me. I'll research the archives of the *Los Angeles Times* or *The Racing Form*. It'll be like having our own key and personalized invitation to the bank vault." I explained my plan further while Hank listened passively.

Finally, he could contain his silence no longer. "You're not taking into consideration the very best part."

"What's that?"

"Many items that are extremely valuable today, could be had for a pittance in 1945."

"What do you mean, Hank? Cars?"

"No, though they would of course be valuable today. But we'll target small collectibles: coins, stamps, baseball cards, even certain comic books. You could win big at the track, but not as much as you wanted. You mustn't draw attention to yourself. Don't think I'm not worried about this happening. I am! You would only be at the track for a few hours each day. The rest of the time including non-race days, you could convert it all into collectibles. Understand?"

"How much do you think we can net out of this Hank?"

"A hundred million wouldn't be an unreasonable guess, John. Converting your winnings into collectibles would multiply the effect, probably at least a hundredfold."

I whistled as I usually did in surprise moments.

"You have to be very careful. What could I do if you wound up in jail? I have to be here to open and close the bridge. Don't forget you're going into the middle of an America at war. You don't understand a lot of the street jargon, styles, social mores or even what made people tick back then. That's another world, John. One you don't really understand. Your work is cut out and you have a lot of learning to do before you go back there again."

"I know I'll have to get my hair cut, Hank. That Woodward guy noticed it right away."

"That's right, John; get one like mine. I've combed it just like this since the early-fifties."

Hank was right. We made up a research list. I would concentrate on the races and secure suitable clothing.

"On your way home tonight, I suggest you stop at Barnes and Noble. You need to learn street slang of the '30s and '40s. They should have something available on this topic. Also, pick up as many music CDs as you can of artists and big band music from that era. I have another thought on this. Pick up a book on sports history. You may find it necessary to talk baseball and football. I know our GIs could detect Nazi soldiers wearing our uniforms by asking them who won the World Series. It didn't matter if they could speak perfect English either. Most American men knew these things."

"Consider it done, Hank!"

———

We pooled our finances. Hank handled the details of buying the old money. He was able to find a lot of hundred dollar bills in prime condition. He also bought them in denominations as low as two dollars, and acquired a multitude of one dollar silver certificates.

I spent one entire evening at the main library in downtown Los Angeles, pulling up the archives of the *L. A. Times*. These were stored on film in the magazine reference section. I scoured the sports pages of each issue for those six weeks I would spend there. I copied all of these race results, took them home and began memorizing. We were going to make a killing. I couldn't risk winning thousands at the track on any single bet. I would have to limit these wins from eight hundred to less than a thousand dollars. I had to be careful not bet too much, too often, at any one window. There was a silver lining here; Santa Anita had dozens of windows. I could place the same bet at many windows, and then alternate these locations for the next race. Picking up a million at the track within those six weeks shouldn't be too hard. I learned that early in 1945 Santa Anita had been converted for military use. They even interned Japanese Americans there for a while. But by May of 1945, it was back in service as a race track. The timing would be perfect.

I would utilize mornings and non-race days buying collectibles. Afternoons would be spent at the track. Hank bought books and magazines and searched the web. From these sources, he worked out a preferred wish list. Everything we acquired would have to be small. The vortex of the machine wasn't large enough for the really big stuff. Many rare coins would bring us ten to one hundred thousand dollars each. These, I would concentrate on most. Like Hank said, once I converted our winnings into collectibles, we could easily net a hundred million here in the present. We couldn't take advantage of stocks or real estate. There would be no way to establish a legal chain of ownership into the present. And I couldn't allow myself to become too well known in that era either. I had to keep all of our assets liquid.

I must have the right clothes and blend in. Hank explained that well dressed men in those days usually always wore hats and suits when they could. It was still that way in the early '50s when he grew into manhood. It wasn't easy finding a good Fedora today that would look right in the mid-1940s. I remembered an old tailor, Ted Goldman. His shop was on Colorado Boulevard in downtown Pasadena. He made all of dad's suits. If Ted was still in business he could do the same for me. My luck held. Ted was there, and he not only remembered my dad, but me as well. I told him what I needed.

He was amused. "Going to a costume ball, John?"

"You might say that, Ted. I joined little social group. We like to dress up in 1940's style when we get together. At these parties, we dance and listen to big band music. Call it nostalgia I guess, but we enjoy stepping back to our grandfather's generation."

"Well, it sounds like fun. I was a boy working in my father's shop during the war, this one right here. I was twelve in 1945. I can make a couple of suits for you. Actually, the changes between then and now are minor. And I got something else, just a minute!" He returned from the back room with a dusty old hat box. Opening it, he pulled out an old but immaculate black Fedora. "Try this on, John."

It fit perfectly! "Ted, how did you do that?"

"Back in the early '50s, an old gentleman who knew my father ordered this hat. I remember the day he came into the shop. My father made all of his suits. We didn't have the hat in his size that day. He insisted on prepaying. And then he never came back. My father didn't know what to do with it, and wouldn't sell it because it belonged to the old gentleman. By and large father forgot about it. It stayed on the shelf all these

years. Until you asked for one just now, I forgot about it too."
Ted chuckled, "I'm beginning to think he's not going come back
and pick it up."

"I'll take it, Ted. How much?"

"One dollar!"

"Did you say one dollar?"

"Yes, it's already been paid for once. Like I said, I don't think
the old gentleman is coming back. Take it and have fun at your
party. I can make you a good suit for $400. Tell you what, two
suits for six hundred and seventy-five and I'll throw in the hat."

I had been lucky with this one. Old Ted was seventy-two
and was going to retire in a couple of months or so.

"I always liked to work, John. But enough is enough, and
now it's my time to move on. I have no son to follow in my footsteps. For three generations, my grandfather, father and I, all of
us were tailors. My grandparents came to the 'States from Riga
when they were in their late forties. My father was the youngest
of eight children. You know, my grandmother never learned to
speak English. Back in the old neighborhood where my dad grew
up, she could get along without it. Father came to California
when I was nine. But all that is gone. I am going to spend more
time with the grandchildren. I have daughters you know."

I thanked him, and we talked about how much the city
had changed. A week later, I went back and picked my suits up.
Trying them on, I couldn't but help smile inwardly; it just gets
better and better. I said goodbye to Ted, knowing that I would
probably never see him again.

I spent the rest of the day going through pawn and antique
shops. I acquired two old valises from the '30s or '40s in good condition. I also bought a good looking old Waltham pocket watch

and chain. I couldn't find the right type of razor and blades. It would take too long to hunt them down. They weren't essential. Back in the '40s, many men went to barber shops to get their shaves. There would be plenty of those around. I couldn't find the right pen either. I would just buy a few things on the other side.

I read news stories from early 1945. I couldn't allow myself to be ignorant of my new surroundings. Who could begin to guess what unknown situation I might have to talk my way out of? This could be critical. Over a six week stretch I would be interacting with a lot of people. Red flags couldn't be allowed to pop up in those people's minds. My biggest weakness is that I tended to be rash. Hank was always thoughtful. Why couldn't I be more like him? But I had my strong point too; my memory was excellent. This was fortunate, because I could not risk taking back written results of things yet to happen.

What about I.D? I couldn't have anything to tie me to the future. One thing for sure, I could not drive back there. I could not risk being in an accident, and no firearms this time. From an old cigar box in my desk I took out my dad's Master Mason Ring. I slipped it on the fourth finger of my right hand, hoping it would fit. My dad and I were about the same size; it did. I had not followed in his footsteps, though that's what he wanted. I knew being a Mason might open doors for me, but I didn't know their words and signs. I have nothing to lose, I thought; it goes with me.

———

Hank finished his master list. We scheduled my departure for Monday morning, next week. "John, take this home and memorize it. I hope you're doing that with those track results. You can't take back anything written with you. I'm guessing if you were caught with this information, the authorities would charge you with fixing races. Then they would wonder where you came from. You do understand how important this is?"

"I'm on the same wavelength. You don't have to worry about me. I'll be so good; you'll be able to call me St. Lander when I get back."

"Ha, ha, ha! Well, St. Lander, I envy you. I wish I could go myself."

"Your day is coming, Hank. Sooner than you think! Know what?"

"What's that, John?"

"The rules might be different where you plan to go. Maybe you won't have to die."

"Doesn't that make you want to go into the future too?"

"I can't think that far ahead. I'm like a train on a track. I go in one direction, one station at a time. But, who knows?"

We discussed the list, especially those dates we were most interested in. I knew I would have to study the list over and over until I could visualize it in my mind. The list was twenty pages long. The first and most important pages were strictly coins. The rest was comprised of other collectibles: comic books, and baseball cards, watches, and stamps, even Faberge eggs! "Can you memorize this within the next five days, John?"

"I'll be ready! I am short of one thing. I have no I.D. What will I do when I'm asked for one?"

"I've considered that, John. It's not a major problem as long as you stay out of trouble. Most people who didn't own property or drive could get along without any I.D. back then. But I do have something for you; wait here." He returned and handed me a faded social security card. It had the name John Dalton Winters on it. "This belonged to my grandfather. He died in 1943. You must only use it if you have to. There was a death certificate on file for him in California in 1945."

"So, I'm going to be John Winters."

"Yes, John; but every person you meet establishes another link in a chain that can be followed back to you. I recommend that you give a different name to each stranger whom you don't expect to see again."

We talked more about our venture. "You have to be self-centered, John. It would be nice to do a few good things. But you can't fundamentally change anything. If you did, right here and right now, you and I talking together like this, might not happen. We are risking that anyway. You get in and get out. That's the way it has to be. Does this make sense to you?"

I agreed! "But look here, Hank; suppose you go into a future where you might not belong. We don't even know if things are going to be more advanced. Civilization might go the other way. Imagine, what if a caveman was brought into our own time? He would be a freak. And one way or another he would be put on display; that is, if he didn't kill somebody first."

"That's right. That's why we explore many different eras of the future. We'll find the right one, a better one, John, much better than 1945!"

"But 1945 is perfect for our purpose. Suppose I had gone way back in time. I'd probably be hung for being strange too. But with information like this in my head, 1945 will be the tree that holds our golden apples. Time could be our playground, Hank. Anyway, let's make the most of it."

He smiled at me and slowly shook his head. Last minute preparations had to be made on the machine. I programmed it so that after I passed through, the bridge would totally close for six weeks in 1945. On Hank's end it would be different. He would begin activation within minutes to recover me after those six weeks. "You realize that we will probably age at different rates, John?"

"I'll trade those few weeks for my share of a cool hundred million," I replied.

We carefully went over the settings for the recall. At the appropriate moment Hank would partially open the bridge and wait for the signal from my beacon. We agreed that if he didn't receive it, he would open up the bridge full at specific intervals, and leave it that way for several minutes. We couldn't risk leaving the bridge even partially opened for that entire time, though I wanted to. It required too much power to open and maintain. The generators were old and they used a lot of fuel. We couldn't risk having them go through excessive mechanical wear or breaking down. With me on the other side, Hank might not be able to patch things up.

Sunday, on the final evening, I stayed at home. I carefully laid out everything that was going back with me on my bed. I inventoried all of it, again and again. It worried me that I might forget something. Together, Hank and I had managed to accumulate over fourteen thousand dollars in old bills and silver dollars. This part hadn't been easy. We really paid through the nose for some of these pieces. Older bills are routinely destroyed by the Feds. We had better luck with silver dollars with common dates like 1922 and 1923. But I couldn't carry many of these. Satisfied that I had everything, I carefully packed my two valises with the money. Then, put a layer of shirts, underwear and socks over it.

I went downstairs to my desk and took out the lists that Hank had prepared for me. One last time I wanted to go over them. I also looked over the race track results again. These were long since etched in my memory. But, one last look for the road. Then I settled down in my easy chair, and poured myself a long shot of bourbon. I looked the lists over and over, closing my eyes, visualizing the writing on the paper. It wasn't long before the strain of concentrating caused my mind to wander. The papers began to blur; I couldn't take anymore strain. I finished my drink and walked up the stairs and into my bedroom. Without stopping I went straight into the bathroom, shredded the paperwork, and flushed it down the toilet. Then, I went to bed, but sleep wouldn't come easy. I tossed and turned. Though tired, my excitement couldn't be contained. Finally, I drifted off to sleep only an hour before the alarm rang.

chapter

6

CHARMAINE

We would be in Darwin within twelve hours and I wanted to be fresh and wide awake when we arrived. I decided to get some sleep. As I closed my eyes, her pretty face was all I could see. Charmaine! Remember that day, John Lander. Remember that day you crossed the time bridge and met Charmaine. I smiled as I drifted off to sleep, dreaming of Charmaine.

Time was at hand. Hank and I went over the checklist. I carefully re-examined the settings. "So long, Hank; see you in six weeks!"

"Good luck, John Lander; see you in a few minutes!"

The whirr of the generators, the falling sensation and I was through. Landing on my feet, I took off the ear muffs and stuffed them in one of the valises. It was strangely cold for May in the

San Fernando Valley. Smudge pots were spread throughout the orchard though not lit. I walked down the middle of the grove so that I wouldn't be spotted by the old couple at the Woodward place. I came out on the other side of the grove and walked down the road toward the gas station that Mr. Woodward told me about. Twenty minutes and one mile later I was there. The attendant told me a local bus would stop there at four. Walking over to the coke machine, I lifted the lid and pulled one out. "How much for a coke?" I asked the owner.

"Five cents, sir."

There were stacks of newspapers by the cash register; I read the nearest headlines as I reached for my wallet. They immediately caught my attention. 'Allies Pressing toward Germany,' it read. "You keep a lot of old papers like this?" I asked.

"No, that's today's issue, mister." The date on the paper was Saturday, November 21, 1944!

Christ! I'm over five months early. The machine's oscilloscope wasn't as precise as we thought. That wavelength covered a range of time. I should have experimented and fine tuned it further. My information won't be any good for another five months. Well, the machine is set to retrieve me in the grove six weeks from now. Hank won't know any better either. It will be six weeks on this end before I can send a recall signal through. I would just have to make the best of it. I picked up copies of all the three major newspapers, and put them on the countertop. "I'll take these papers too, sir."

The proprietor charged me three cents apiece for them. I recognized the *Los Angeles Times* but I had never heard of the *Los Angeles Herald* and the *Los Angeles Mirror*. I would get settled in and look at their classifieds later.

This was Chatsworth, a pretty little farm region covered by orange and lemon groves in 1944. The efficient red car system didn't come out this far. But the bus would go right down Topanga Canyon Road from here, into Canoga Park and then follow Victory into Burbank. I knew my way around Burbank some. I would spend the night there. Enough people lived there so that I could blend in without attracting too much attention. And it might be easier getting a room in the suburbs, than in downtown L.A.

At twenty minutes to five, I stepped off the bus in Burbank. I was able to secure a second floor room in an old hotel on Victory Boulevard. I paid two days in advance and stowed my valises under the bed in my room. Monday, I would look for more suitable lodging. Making sure I had plenty of money with me, I went back down the stairs. All eyes were on me as I walked through the hotel's lobby. The folks sitting around were looking me over. Ted did too good a job on my suit; I was overdressed for this place. It was apparent that most of these people lived here and the lobby was their gathering place to socialize. Pipe and cigar smoke filled the room and everybody seemed acquainted. That was fine, I thought, but they won't get to know me. Still, I wondered what impression I made with them.

Out on the sidewalk, I followed Victory Boulevard toward its busier end. I didn't have far to go until I came upon a bar. This was a good start, just what I wanted; I ducked inside. It was smoke filled and loaded with servicemen, a few guys in suits, and several blue collar types. The big Lockheed Plant was only blocks away, and this would be the first stop for many after the day shift. Intermingled among them were women of all ages. The conversation was lively. From the juke box, the tune *Long Ago and Far Away* permeated the room. I was thankful Hank made me familiarize myself with the music of the '30s and '40s. Many years had passed since I was in a place this smoky. I took a vacant stool to the right of a shapely blonde and nodded to the bartender as he came over. "Is this a revival meeting?" I asked.

The bartender laughed. "Sure, what can I get for you?"

"Thank God, I was afraid it was a drinking establishment. Bring me a beer; no make it two, just in case you get real busy."

"A two fisted drinker, eh." The bartender returned with two bottles. "Here you are, buddy." He sat one down, then tipped the glass and started to pour the other.

I looked at the bottle, Acme beer, whoever heard of this? "Whoa! Just set it down and pour it straight up. Good beer has to have a head on it."

"Here, you pour it, buddy! That'll be thirty cents."

My taste buds didn't exactly agree with Acme beer. I longed for the girlfriend in the green dress. But these people would never have heard of a Heineken in 1944. I laid a dollar on the bar. I took another long swallow and looked around. The young blonde sitting next to me was trying to ignore advances from a serviceman sitting on her left. She put a cigarette to her lips, turned to me and shoved her matches in my direction.

"How about a light, mister?" She was about twenty-two with that peek-a-boo Veronica Lake style of hair.

"Sure, baby; I'll light your fire!" I picked up her matches, struck one and leaned it toward her as she put a cigarette to her lips.

The blonde smiled at me, "You don't waste much time, do you?"

"I get acquainted real fast, honey."

"Oh, aren't you are the cute one, a slicker too!" This gal wasn't afraid to spar with me.

I wondered what a slicker was, but didn't want to ask. "Call me John. My name is John Winters."

"John, well that's nice," she said with a forced smile.

"Know what cutie? You really should go out with me sometime."

"Oh, why?" she replied indifferently.

"Well, I'd wine and dine you. And besides, I like the way you fill up the curves of that dress. Now that's something I'd like to look further into. I'd show you a real good time."

The blonde laughed hysterically. "I haven't had this much fun in a long time. What makes you think I'd go out with you?"

"Baby, have you had a better offer today?"

The blonde replied thoughtfully, "No, you move fast!"

"My heart has ticked at least half of its beats, baby; when they put down the lid I don't get any more chances." I had her attention. Briefly, I thought about my promise to Hank. Hell, there's nothing wrong with just flirting. Besides, he has ice water in his veins. I'm red-blooded.

The bartender walked to the far corner of the bar near the door as a couple of young Hispanics walked in. "Get out; we don't want no greasers in here!"

The larger of the two men protested. "My brother is already in the Navy and I got my draft notice too."

"I don't care," the bartender replied. More yelling followed. Some of the Anglo servicemen verbally backed up the bartender. The Latinos were intimidated. A few other Anglos didn't seem so happy about it, but they remained silent.

The second Hispanic said, "*Olvides, Manuel; este cabron es hijo de una puta!*"

"*De Veras, Julio; chingale. Vamonos!*"

More words were exchanged between them and the bartender, hostile ones. Before long, they left the bar. I had never thought about race relations in California back in the 1940s. I tuned the episode out.

I turned my attention back to the blonde. She was trying to be cheerful but I could see she was haunted by something. "Want a drink? What's your name?"

"Charmaine, Charmaine Lund and the answer is yes. You make me laugh and I could use some cheering up anyway." I had her attention. She seemed uninterested in all of the young servicemen in the bar. Why me, a man approaching middle age? Was she a hooker? As time passed on I put that out of my head. This young woman wasn't at all sophisticated and she wasn't used to booze either. The small talk flowed easy between us. I was a flirt but she didn't seem threatened by me as she had with the young serviceman. The girl was trying to pound her drinks down faster than she could handle them. Her words were beginning to slur.

An hour passed; I was getting hungry. Besides this, I wanted to sober this girl up. "How about a bite to eat, Charmaine?"

"That would be nice. I haven't eaten all day."

"Good, you need some food. You've had enough to drink. Can we walk to a good place from here?"

"There's a small place called the Victory Cafe, right here on the boulevard. It's not far. We can walk there in minutes. But they don't serve drinks."

"That's OK; I'll live. The Victory Cafe it is!" I raised my glass, and smiled at her. "Here's to your big blue eyes." Somewhat unsteady, she clung to me and I guided her as we left the bar and walked outside.

The Victory Café was a small place, not much more than a coffee shop. I could tell Charmaine hadn't been to very many nice restaurants. Actually, I hadn't seen any here that would compare to the world of 2007. But the little Victory was popular. People were constantly going in and out.

Over hamburgers and fries, Charmaine regained some sobriety. We had a few laughs over dinner, and lingered long afterwards over coffee. Though I didn't like cigarettes, I took pleasure in lighting hers. Until today, this was something I hadn't done for a woman in years.

It was pretty clear that neither of us wanted to leave. It was my impression that she had been lonely for some time now. This made no sense; she was a knockout. I always had my share of feminine companionship, but there was a certain electricity here I had never quite experienced before. From her body language, I could see she must have felt something too. She was exciting, and this evening was progressing nicely. Our mutual animal attraction was so spontaneous a blind man could have seen it. I turned on my charm; hers came naturally. What about my promise to Hank? Well, let's see; I made that promise in 2007 and it's only 1944. OK, so I haven't made it yet. All's fair!

Late that evening Lander woke up in Charmaine's apartment; their lovemaking had been intense just a couple of hours before. He looked at his watch; four hours had elapsed since they left the Victory. Charmaine slowly roused and snuggled close to him. Lander got up, went to the small bathroom, ran some water and washed his face. Returning, there sat Charmaine lighting a cigarette.

"You know, those things will kill you some day."

"I'm a big girl and nobody ever told me that before. You're one the few guys I ever met who doesn't smoke. How come?"

"Special knowledge, Charmaine, though I did when I was young. Someday that will all change, and there won't be many public places where you can smoke. It's the worst thing you can do to yourself. Think on that one, pretty baby!"

"I never heard anything like that before in my life. Anyway, when do I get to know more about the man that walked into a girl's life this evening? You are so different from anyone I ever met before."

Lander had been evading these personal questions all evening. "Tell me about yourself, Charmaine; what do you do for a living?"

"I work at the Lockheed plant here in Burbank five evenings a week on the swing shift, sometimes Saturdays too. It's only three blocks from here. I was raised by my grandparents on their farm in Wisconsin. My papa died in an accident in a railroad switching yard where he worked in Racine. I was only ten when mama left me and my older sister with grandma and grandpa Lund. She went to Madison and got a job there. She planned to eventually support us herself. It was tough to get a decent job in the depression. She couldn't care for us and still work. But then mama caught pneumonia and died. We became orphans.

My grandparents are nice but I couldn't wait to grow up and get away on my own. And then the war came. My older sister's family lives out here in L.A. She and her husband Tom invited me to come and stay with them. That was OK for a while, but Tom is so old fashioned. And I wanted freedom. I got this job at the Lockheed plant, you see, and the money is good. I was so lonely last night but then I met you. I never knew anybody like you. How come you're not in the service?"

"I'm thirty-six, Charmaine; they probably wouldn't want me anyway. Besides, I have important business."

"Businessman, I knew it! You don't look thirty-six. You don't talk much about yourself; do you, John? You never told me where you lived. What kind of business are you in anyway?"

I started to feel the walls close in around me. I am on a mission but have yielded to the natural attraction and impulse I feel anytime I'm near a good looking woman. Is this lovely creature trying to bond with me? There's not a rope long enough or scaffold high enough to hang me from. What have I done? I'm just an interloper who has come back in time for selfish reasons. What kind of damage have I done? How many futures have I changed? "Known many guys, Charmaine?"

Feeling the silence I turned around. Charmaine was silently weeping. I experienced a wave of guilt. I walked toward the bed. "Don't take it so hard, I didn't mean anything by it."

She turned away from me. "You think I'm cheap, and I probably am. I haven't been out anywhere around town for six months. My fiancé, a marine, was killed somewhere in the Pacific and I was lonely. I just wanted to be around people. And then you came in."

I walked around to her side of the bed, sat down and gently embraced her. Without saying a word I slowly rocked her back and forth, and then she exploded in a burst of sobbing. Overcome with a wave of emotion above my waist, I said to her, "Tomorrow is Sunday, why don't you spend the day with me and we'll have a few laughs."

She reached up and clung to me desperately. "OK," she softly said.

"It's getting late, Charmaine. I had better go now."

"Stay with me."

The next morning, Sunday, Charmaine made me eggs and toast with coffee. I sat at the small table in her one room apartment, and she put my plate in front of me. Before seating herself across from me, she took a large white chunk of some substance I didn't recognize, and put it in a pan. Then, she opened a packet and emptied the contents in with it, and began stirring them together until the substance turned yellow.

"What is that, Charmaine?"

"Margarine," she said, with a surprised look from my question. "I'll have it ready for you in a second."

"Margarine! That stuff is nasty. Don't you have any butter?"

She stopped stirring. "What's nasty about it; butter is rationed."

Then I remembered reading about this in school, ration cards; of course. "Charmaine, I'm going to eat my toast dry; you should do the same."

"I don't understand you, John."

"The molecules in margarine are chemically speaking, almost a plastic. It's made from hydrogenated vegetable oil, which causes all kind of health problems. I've been told that bugs won't even touch it."

"I never heard that before. What is a molecule?"

"Charmaine, didn't you study that in school?"

"I heard of them, yeah; it has something to do with science. Doesn't it? Johnny, I went to a three room country school in Wisconsin. By the way, I prefer butter too. I guess I have a lot of the farm girl still inside me."

An idea formed in my mind. It would be easier to operate with an associate. She had an I.D. That might become important someday. She knew a few people, and I would be less conspicuous with a lady for a companion. Besides, she was a bonus I didn't want to let pass through my lecherous fingers. I wouldn't tell Hank; he would be furious. Hell, Hank could walk into a whorehouse with a thousand dollar bill in his pocket and still not get laid. "How would you like to work for me? I will pay you $100 per week, plus living expenses and a bonus too. How about it?"

"You would pay me $100 a week! Doing what?

"As my assistant, my secretary!"

Her eyes opened wide as she softly raised her eyebrows in wonder. "I've never worked as a secretary. I don't know shorthand or how to type."

"It's OK, Charmaine; never mind all that. You have qualities that I value much more."

She blushed. "There's more to me than that, John."

"I know it, honey. Don't let your pretty feelings get hurt over it."

"But I work at the aircraft plant, and the war is still on. That wouldn't be right. Yesterday, before I met you at the bar, I was thinking about joining the WACs."

"The war is almost over, Charmaine. Believe me, honey; you won't be missed. But I would miss you." I lowered my gaze to her leg with intense interest as the hem of her robe slid off, revealing her snow white thigh.

Aware of my attention, she blushed. "I'm not just a piece of flesh you know."

"I already know that, baby. The prettiest part of you lies between your ears. But it comes nicely packaged." I reached my hand across the table to her. "It's just so easy; that's why we're made of flesh, so we can enjoy each other. We didn't make these rules, so we don't have to think about things so deeply. Charmaine, this is our now time; moments like this don't always come again. Let's live this for all it's worth?"

She looked back at me with warm, bedroom eyes and slowly stood up. Untying her robe she let it slip to the floor. I rose and took this snow goddess in my arms.

She closed her eyes. "Kiss me. Kiss me as much as you like," she whispered. I pressed my lips against hers as my tongue gently searched for hers. Her eyes opened wide. I could see she had never been kissed like this before. Charmaine responded eagerly; then she melted in my arms as her tongue met mine. I scooped her up in my arms and carried her to the bed. It was a very good morning indeed!

Later that morning as she snuggled in my arms, we chatted. It was uncanny, but I felt so comfortable with her, like I had known her all my life. We had not even been together twenty-four hours, yet somehow, she was no stranger. I asked her if she had thought about her future, now that the war was almost over.

"Johnny, how do you know the war is almost over? You just seem to know so much."

"Yes, baby; I'm a real live know it all." I decided to change the subject. "Do you have a driver's license?"

"Yes. I used to help grandpa on the farm. He taught me how to drive. He has a Chevy truck, and he hauled a lot of hay. You see, grandpa has milk cows. I even got to drive his Ford tractor sometimes. Grandma Lund didn't like it; she's so old fashioned. I didn't get my driver's license until I moved to California. My brother-in-law Tom let me use his car once in a while, until I moved out. So I took the written test and got one."

Written test, I thought. "Good, we'll get a car tomorrow. You'll get a car," I corrected myself. "And we will get a bigger place with a telephone."

"John, I can't afford a car right now." She paused, suddenly surprised. "Do you mean that we are going to live together?"

"Yes, Charmaine; we're going to play house. And don't worry about the car; I'll do all the affording. You are my permanent designated driver."

"Johnny, this is such a whirlwind thing between us. Now I know how Dorothy must have felt in the Wizard of Oz. I feel like I've been swept up by the wind and taken to another world. Yet, somehow, I don't care. Don't you know how to drive?"

Uncomfortable with the question, I decided to change the subject. "I need to concentrate on other things."

Sunday was spent getting acquainted with my new companion. I knew it was worth coming back here just to meet her. It fleetingly occurred to me that I was changing someone's future. But I didn't care. I wanted her for myself for as long as I was here. Have a conscience, Lander. Well, I might even grow one someday, but first things first. I told Charmaine to pretty herself up while I took care of some business.

I walked to a barber shop on Victory, not far from the hotel I had checked into yesterday. I forgot this was Sunday; it was closed. There was a little market on the corner. I walked inside and bought a razor and some blades.

As I walked outside a young boy approached me. "Paper, mister? Want to buy a paper?"

I took one as I gave the boy a quarter. "Keep the change. What's your name, lad?"

"Russ," he replied.

"Russ, if you or your friends want to make a little extra money, I buy old baseball cards and comic books."

"You do?" he answered.

"Yes, I do."

"I got lots of friends. I'll ask around. I always hang around here before I go to school in the morning. Mister Davis lets me sell papers in front of his store."

"I'll see you within a couple of days, Russ. Remember to tell your friends!"

"I will, mister!"

I went back to the hotel where I picked up my valises. I checked out, telling the manager to forget the extra day's rent. Then, I carried my goods over the short distance back to Charmaine's place. I freshened up with a shower and change of clothes. Within the next half hour, we walked to the red car stop. I held her hand as we waited there. "Charmaine baby, do these cars go to the beach?"

"I think so, Johnny. The conductor can tell us."

We didn't have long to wait until one stopped. The conductor told us which line to take, and I bought two interchange tickets for Santa Monica. The city looked so strange to me, no freeways. The red car quickly covered the distance and we got off in Santa Monica.

It was a sunny day, yet cool and nice in late November. I wanted to walk by the water. There we were, barefoot on the beach, talking, and holding hands. Being with Charmaine was the most fun I'd had in years. It turned out that she was twenty-one. But she made me feel eighteen. Did I dare let myself fall too deeply for her? I was a man of the future. But did I have the willpower to resist? I couldn't begin to guess what alternate reality I might be creating. I didn't care. Charmaine was responding the same way to me as she shared her innermost thoughts. I realized she had a certain innocence I wasn't used to. One thing was apparent; she didn't hesitate to place her trust in me. This girl could easily be hurt. I must be careful with her feelings. Temporarily, I forgot why I had traveled to this far place in time. The flames burned bright within me that afternoon. This was my time, and I was going to make the most of it.

Later that afternoon after lunch, I took Charmaine for a walk through the neighborhood. I never remembered seeing anything like this in my own time. Kids! Kids everywhere! Boys were playing football in the streets. Little boys were running around playing cowboys and Indians. Girls were playing jacks and hopscotch on the sidewalks. Kids were roller skating and riding their bikes! Adults were rocking in swings on their porches. Strange, I wonder if these people would trade all of this for video games, TVs and computers. The world stood still for me that afternoon. I had no mission. There was no past, no future, only now. In a moment's madness I even considered; I could easily live here. No, I'm going to make it big and go back to my electronic world. And I'm going in style.

That evening after we cleaned up at Charmaine's little apartment, I went to a phone booth nearby and called for a cab. We were waiting on the sidewalk when it arrived. We got in. "Please take us to Hollywood, to the Brown Derby," I told the cab driver.

"You got it, Hollywood and the Brown Derby!" I knew Charmaine liked to see celebrities.

Before we got out of the Burbank, an idea hit me. "Driver, is Tam O' Shanters still in Glendale?"

"What da ya mean, still in Glendale? It's right there where it's always been. Right on Los Feliz."

"Take us there instead."

"Awright, mister!" I could see he wasn't happy. I had just cut his pay. He brightened up later when I gave him a two dollar tip.

Tam O' Shanters had been a favorite of me and Monica. That evening, over steaks and wine, I heard raucous laughter and a familiar voice from around the corner. I had to see for myself. I knew the Tam had been an early hangout for the Hollywood crowd. I told Charmaine I would be right back. I stood up and walked a few steps so I could see for myself. Sure enough, there he was, at a smoke filled table in the corner.

He saw me too and bellowed out, "Come on over here, pardner, so I can get a good look at you too." I did and realized as he shook my hand, how down to Earth and cordial he really was. He looked at me with that shoulder to shoulder grin that I remembered from so many of his old movies. It was always a big deal with my dad to watch the old cowboy reruns on Sunday morning. I often watched these with him, until I became too sophisticated for them. Or was I? He offered me a drink. I declined. He introduced me to the cluster of people around the table; some whose faces I vaguely remembered from the old westerns. "My lady would like to meet you," I said.

"Bring 'er on." Flirting came easy to him; he took Charmaine's hand. "What's a good lookin' gal like you doin' with this mug?" Charmaine was in heaven. "Is she your wife, pardner?"

"No, she is my main squeeze!"

"Ha, ha, ha! I could squeeze some of that maself!" After a few more flirtatious exchanges he started looking away, and I could see he wanted to get back with his own friends. "I'm gettin' mighty envious, pardner; better get her away while you can." That was our cue to go. This was all Charmaine could talk about for the rest of the evening.

Monday, I waited at the gate of the Lockheed plant in Burbank until Charmaine returned. She had handed in her resignation. "They're not very happy about this, Johnny! I can't believe I'm doing it either. It's not like me." She stood before me, head slightly tilted, staring at me with the strangest expression. It seemed like a long time before she spoke. "Johnny, I feel like I've stood here before, looking at you just like this. I don't know what's come over me. I just feel like I would go anywhere with you."

I didn't dwell on it then, I wanted to move on. Later I realized she had a déjà vu moment of her own. I took her by the hand. "Come on, Charmaine baby; we have things to do!" I was

thinking ahead. It's time to put this plan in action. I came back
here to make money. I grabbed her hand as we went to the red
car stop nearby, and waited for a car to Glendale. Riding these
red cars was becoming tiresome. I didn't want to plan my activities around a train schedule. It was a short ride to Glendale. As
we sat on the train I handed her the classifieds from the *Times
Mirror*. I looked at those in the *L.A. Times*. "We have to get a set
of wheels, baby. Let's see what's available. I don't want to spend
all day long changing trains just to move around town."

"Don't we need something to put a set of wheels on, Johnny?
I don't understand."

I sighed. "Sorry, sweetie; I wasn't thinking in today's terms.
We need a car."

"Today's terms? I wonder what tomorrow's terms are going
to be?"

"That's just the way I sometimes think and talk." She took
my hand and smiled. We got off the red car in Glendale and sat
on the waiting bench reading the ads.

"Johnny, look at this. There's a 1938 DeSoto for sale right
here in Glendale."

"Let me see that, honey? It's on Broadway. There's an address
but no phone number. If I remember right, that's not too far
from here. Come on, baby; we'll stretch our legs."

It was a chance thing. Early in the day it was uncertain if
anyone would be home. We walked up the steps and I knocked
on the door. Soon it was answered by an elderly man.

He was somewhat grouchy. "What do you folks want?"

"Do you have a DeSoto for sale, sir?"

"Yes."

"How much do you want for it?"

"A hundred and twenty-five," he responded.

"Could we see it please?"

"It's in the garage; I'll back it out. Just a minute while I go inside and get the keys." Minutes later the old man was backing the brown DeSoto out of his single car garage. He left the engine running as he raised the hood. I looked at the engine. It hummed with a steady purr. I walked around it. Except for a small dent in the left rear fender it was pretty clean. It had a long hood and a running board. The upholstery was brown and a little dingy but was intact and clean.

"It has a radio too," the old man said.

All I could think of to say was, "Cool."

He stared at me. "What do you mean by cool?"

"I don't mean anything by it, sir. Why are you selling the car?"

Frowning, he cleared his throat. "I don't see so good anymore. I bought this car new. There ain't nothin' wrong with it that I know of. I always changed the oil ever three thousand miles myself."

"Well, it looks clean," I replied.

Charmaine gently tugged on my arm, and then whispered in my ear. "Offer him seventy-five, Johnny."

I looked at the older man squarely. "I'll give you seventy-five."

He hesitated with a sour expression before replying. "A hundred, I won't go no lower."

"Deal," I replied! We followed him into his house and waited at the kitchen table for him to bring the pink slip. I told him to sign it over to Charmaine Lund.

"How much did you pay for insurance on this car, sir?"

"Insurance? I don't carry no insurance. Hardly anybody I know does."

"How soon before Miss Lund has to register it in her name?"

"Oh, I think it's about fifteen days. But it doesn't much matter if she goes beyond that." I gave him a hundred dollar bill. He took some things out of the trunk and glove compartment.

Charmaine backed the car out onto Broadway and headed it toward Colorado Boulevard. This should work really well I thought. The DeSoto won't attract any attention. Attention is just what I don't need. We turned onto Colorado Boulevard heading toward Burbank. Soon we crossed Brand and came to Central. We passed a large brick apartment building at the corner of Central and Colorado, on the same site the Galleria would occupy many years later. My eye caught the sign in the window. Vacancy, it read.

"Charmaine, swing around the block." She glanced at me with a puzzled look. "I think we just found a new home, honey," I reassured her. The apartment was fully furnished, larger and nicer than Charmaine's. It had a separate kitchen. The bath was just that, one of those large tubs so common in those days. The bed swung down out of the wall. This was something I had only seen in the movies. "Look at this Charmaine." Then my tongue accidentally slipped. "I've only seen these in old movies." I hoped she would overlook it.

She gave me a puzzled look. "Yes, Johnny, a Murphy bed; it will give us more room. And look; we have an ironing board that swings out of the wall too!"

"You're not going to be doing much ironing, baby!" I registered us as Mr. and Mrs. John Winters and gave the manager three months rent in advance.

Then I decided we would go downtown. "Let's go to L.A."

"What are we going to do there?"

"Business, Charmaine!"

"So, I get to see what Mr. Winters does for a living. Am I your secretary today or your girlfriend?" she asked with a tease.

"A little of both, baby. I might do some buying, and we'll have a little fun there too."

She steered the DeSoto away from the curve and headed it south on Central. "What road do I follow from here, Johnny?"

"Let's see; keep going until we reach San Fernando Road, just a few blocks from here. Take a left when we get there; it will take us downtown. I think. And we can turn on Alameda from there." I had to reconstruct in my mind these city streets. I was used to thinking in terms of freeways. We almost made it out of Glendale before the DeSoto had a flat tire. I didn't want to risk this happening again. Working up a sweat in my new tailor made suit wasn't what I had in mind when I came back here. Tires were a problem in 1944. All civilians could get were recaps and used tires. I took off my coat, rolled up my sleeves and changed out the flat. The spare looked as sorry as the one I had removed. "Charmaine?"

"Yes, Johnny?"

"Have we even had this car for one hour? This isn't going to work. I saw a garage on Los Feliz yesterday, when we were going to the Tam. Drive over there."

I knew what I wanted. The mechanic at the garage said he could fix me up if the money was right. I agreed, and he made the necessary call. It was pricey, but I managed to get a set of brand new boot leg tires. They cost me more than the car did. We were stuck at the garage three hours waiting for them to be delivered. I didn't dare guess what kind of government vehicle they had been stolen from. I didn't really care. My personal mission was at least as important as World War II.

———

It was early afternoon before we got to downtown L.A. Traffic on these roads was heavy, but nothing like the nightmare of rush hour freeway traffic I was used to. "Charmaine, turn here; we'll park at Union Terminal and get some lunch close by." Union Terminal was the big passenger train station. In 1944, it was still new. We parked and I took her by the hand as we crossed Alameda and walked along the sidewalk toward the downtown business district. I recognized a sign. "Come on, honey; let's go in here." I forgot this place existed until I saw that sign; then, I remembered. Dad brought me here on those rare occasions when business took him downtown. It's still here! That's funny; I won't be born until 1971, and I think of it as still here. Philippe's was busy just as it would be many years later. Seeing familiar places like this reassured me. I felt like I was just around the block and not sixty-three years away from my own reality in time. I had always liked Phillipe's. There was standing room only inside. The morning's activity must have taxed our appetites. We devoured our pastrami sandwiches.

Before long we were walking down Main Street. Los Angeles was a thriving, bustling city in 1944, not anything like I remembered from my own time. Nothing looked run down. The heart of the city in 1944 was just that; the shops teemed with goods, even in wartime. People hustled and bustled along the street as we blended into the downtown scenery. Soon we were standing in front of a store window. I was looking at some old coins in a window display. "Let's go in here, Charmaine."

"Johnny, this is only a pawn shop. What are you looking for here?"

"You never know what might be in there. We just might find a goldmine of sorts."

We walked in and approached the man behind the cash register. He nodded toward me in recognition. "Can I be of help to you folks?" he said without smiling

"I'm a collector. I buy old coins, stamps and other artifacts. I'm also interested in baseball cards, comic books, jewelry and anything else that might catch my eye."

"Well, you came to right place, Mark Cohen at your service. Just a minute and I'll be right back."

I watched him walk into the back room and open a chest high safe. He returned with several covered trays which he laid on the countertop. As he uncovered them I saw an array of older coins in various stages of wear and condition. Like a sidewinder missile homing in on its target my eyes were immediately attracted to certain ones. Charmaine drifted about looking at other things. She finally stood glancing at a jewelry case not far away. I reached for a 1916 D Mercury dime in mint condition. "How much for this one, Mr. Cohen?"

He quoted his price as I looked at his poker face. I knew he was trying to screw me.

"I'll take it!" We made several such transactions for small denomination coins including two 1909 S VDB pennies in extra fine condition. And I also acquired some gold double eagles fairly cheap, even for those times. I performed some quick math in my head, a cool fifty thousand at least. Hank will be pleased. "How about the other collectibles I had in mind, Mr. Cohen?"

"I don't carry junk like that. But I'm sure I can get you some. What did you say your name was?"

"I didn't, but it's John Moses." This was the first time I had followed Hank's instructions about constantly changing my name.

The name caught his attention. "Jewish?" he asked.

"No, but I don't know much about my family history."

"Look here, Mr. Moses; check back with me in about a week. I'll look around for you."

"Fair enough, see you in about a week, Mr. Cohen." It would prove my salvation later that I didn't keep that appointment and that I changed my name. Cohen and I mutually acknowledged each other with a nod as we walked out of his shop. I looked back and could see that he was smiling at us as he chewed on an unlit cigar.

Charmaine tucked her arm around mine as we strolled away. She looked perplexed. "Johnny, why did you tell him your last name was Moses?"

"Just routine business, Charmaine. Cohen is a pawnbroker. He is probably alright. But I just spent five hundred dollars in his shop, and don't know for sure. He probably has me pegged as a big time collector, which is true. I don't want to leave a trail for anyone's shady associates to follow and try to rip me off later. You'll hear me use other names also."

"What does rip off mean, Johnny? Cheat?"

"In this case, baby, it means steal. What time is it?"

She looked at her watch. "Oh, I don't know; this old thing stopped running."

"Did you wind it this morning, Charmaine?"

"Yes, I always do."

"I think I can do something about that. See that jewelry shop over there; let's go inside." Slightly later that afternoon, Charmaine had a brand new Swiss watch on her wrist.

"You shouldn't have, Johnny; first the car, now this." She held up her wrist admiring it. "It's so pretty!"

"Charmaine, you add to its beauty, not the other way around."

"Still, Johnny, I love it!"

"There's one thing I can think of that would look better on you."

"What's that, Johnny?"

"Me!"

She blushed and looked down. "You embarrass me, Johnny. But I like it."

"Buying you nice things comes easy, Charmaine. I love seeing your face light up."

"You don't seem to care about money, Johnny!"

"Don't worry, you're worth it." I had a moment of remorse thinking about Hank. I knew he wouldn't approve of the way I was using some of the money. What the hell, a little bit of it won't be missed. We're going to make tens of millions. He'll never know.

Before we returned to Glendale late that afternoon, Charmaine wanted to pick up her things in Burbank. We entered her apartment and she set about getting some essentials. "How much time do you need, Charmaine?"

"About a half hour, Johnny. I'm just going to get what I need most. I'll get the junk another time."

I had second thoughts. I didn't want to come back here. "Charmaine, let's get everything this trip. Tell your landlord you're checking out for good. Let's don't leave any loose ends here."

"I don't have any boxes, Johnny."

"Just organize your things. I'll walk down to the little market and get some for you." It was a short walk there. I went inside and the proprietor was able to fix me up with a half dozen cardboard boxes that weren't too bulky for me to carry. Walking back outside, I saw Russ, the paperboy. I knew I should check tomorrow's classifieds. "Have any papers today, Russ?"

"Naw! I sold 'em all. But remember what you said about the comics, mister. My friend Tommy wants to show you his."

"Where is he now, Russ?"

"He lives just a few houses from here."

"I'll be back in about an hour. Why don't you go and ask Tommy to meet me here?" I gave the boy a quarter and his face brightened considerably.

"About an hour. Sure, mister. I'll go get him now."

Back at the apartment, there was a knock on her door. Charmaine opened it. Her landlady handed her some envelopes. "Here's your mail, Charmaine, my dear."

"Thank you, Mrs. Landry. I was going to stop and see you anyway. I'm moving out today."

"What's the matter, Charmaine? Is anything wrong here?"

"No, Mrs. Landry; you're very sweet. There's this fella you see, and I want to be near him."

"Well, my dear, I'm glad you got over that tragedy, your poor Marine. That was awful. I was worried about you these last months. My dear, you still have over three weeks rent on the books. I don't think the owner will let me refund it. Are you sure you want to do this?"

Charmaine smiled and hugged her. "Mrs. Landry, you've always been so sweet to me. I don't care about the money."

"All right, my dear; don't worry about cleaning the place up. I'll have that taken care of. Charmaine, you look happy. I haven't seen you this look this way in a long time. You take good care of yourself dear."

"I'll never forget you, Mrs. Landry. Before I leave, I'll drop the key off to you."

"I'm going out now. Please slide it under my door. Goodbye and I hope good things come to you." They embraced again and Mrs. Landry left.

I got back to Charmaine's place; she was softly sobbing. "What's wrong, baby?"

"Nothing, Johnny; I just said goodbye to my landlady. She was always a friend to me." Charmaine hugged me. "Johnny, this is so sudden; will you always be nice to me?"

I kissed her forehead and tip of her nose. "Are you afraid?"

"A little, I'm sorry. I can't help it."

I ran my tongue over her upper and lower lips as she shuddered from its tickle. She stopped crying and looked in my eyes. I kissed her. "Our future is waiting outside that door, Charmaine. Let's go for it. Drape your clothes in the back seat of the DeSoto and they won't get wrinkled. We'll put the small items in these boxes and get most of them in the trunk."

Within the best part of an hour we had the DeSoto loaded. Charmaine closed the door of the little apartment and slid the key under Mrs. Landry's door. We drove away.

"Charmaine, let's go to that little market near here. There's a boy there I want to talk to."

"Good, I need a few things anyway."

In next to no time we pulled alongside the curb and parked. Waiting there on the sidewalk were Russ and another little boy, younger and a full head shorter than him. Charmaine came around to the sidewalk and paused by my side. "Go get what you need, honey. I want to talk to these boys." She went inside. "Is this your friend, Russ?"

"Yeah, this is Tommy Thompson. Show him, Tommy; show him what you got."

Hesitantly, the little boy handed me a stack of comic books. I started thumbing through them. Many dated from the thirties. Suddenly I stopped. I was holding an original copy of issue number one of *Superman*. Hank discovered one of these had sold for $75,000. And that was a few years before my departure. Others in the stack were worth a small fortune too. Without any hesitation I pulled out my wallet. "How much would you like for this one, Tommy?"

He was shy and cast his eyes downward. "A quarter. If that's too much, I can sell it for less, mister."

I smiled at him. He probably just wanted to pick up a little money for candy. I reached into my wallet, fished inside it until I found a twenty, and handed it to him. "Here, Tommy, does this work?"

He stared at me in disbelief. "You mean it?"

"Take it, Tommy; I want you to have it."

"You want the others? You can have them too, mister."

"Thanks, Tommy; we've got a deal. Shake?" He took my hand and shook it like he was pumping water.

Little Russ just stared in amazement until Tommy grabbed him by the arm. "Come on, Russ. I'll buy you a soda!"

The boys ran inside as Charmaine walked out. "I bought some steaks, honey. I'll make you a good supper tonight."

In our new apartment, I watched her working in the kitchen as I glanced up from the classifieds. I still had those three papers I bought last Saturday in Chatsworth. I had never been around any woman like her. What was that she said to me after she came out of the Lockheed plant in Burbank? I remember, 'I just feel like I would go anywhere with you.' Charmaine was charming and spontaneous, a breath of fresh air. Sure, I'd had many women in my thirty-six years, many girlfriends; I even married two of them. I didn't know what a Charmaine could be until I had one. She was content to be who she was. She could care less about challenging a man's role in the world, and would have made a lousy poster girl for the bra burners one generation later. She was total feminity at its best. Most of all, she's mine for as long as I like! I smiled.

Our apartment in Glendale was right off the business district. After supper that night we walked around town, looking in all the store windows. This was the Christmas season and shoppers were making the most of their time. Of course, there were servicemen everywhere. Charmaine attracted her fair share of looks from them. Too bad guys, she's off limits.

Across the street was the Alexander, a rather elegant looking theatre on Brand Boulevard. We read the marquee. Charmaine wanted to go and have a closer look. Standing in front of the billboard, I could see she wanted to see the movie as she looked at Bette Davis' picture. Yesterday, Sunday, in Santa Monica, she had shared so many of her pretty thoughts with me. I knew she and her sister liked to hang out in front of the studios when they could, watching actors come and go. For her, it was one of the many joys of living in Southern California.

"Come on, baby; we have to see this one." Her excitement bubbled as we took our seats inside. I had seen this old black and white flick as a rerun on TV many years before. That's funny, I marveled, many years before. But tonight, it was like seeing it for the first time. Her excitement became mine also. During those tense moments of drama in the picture, she would squeeze my hand; and that was just fine with me. I don't think she consciously realized it though. She was living in that black and white world on the big screen in front of her. Charmaine was with them.

Over the next three weeks, Charmaine would prove indispensable to me. Daily, she helped me go through the papers; especially productive were the estate sales. I was able to pick up an original Colt Peacemaker in premium condition. It had a low serial number. Potentially, this was worth over a hundred thousand dollars itself. I was able to go through many old coin jars. There was no shortage of good stuff, I could pick and choose. I only bought the best. One of them yielded a 1943 copper penny, worth more than a hundred grand in my time. I didn't waste my time with stamps. Hunting them down was too labor intensive.

Most mornings just after the banks opened, I would go into the ones near by and convert a measure of cash into rolls of coins. I brought these back to the apartment. Charmaine and I would go through them looking for key dates in extra fine condition. Every day I found numerous pennies, nickels, dimes, quarters and halves that would be worth several hundred dollars apiece in 2007. Usually, I only kept those that would net us in excess of a thousand percent profit. Many would tip the scale at ten-thousand per cent. I couldn't wait to see Hank's face. Hank, you're pretty smart alright. This is our private lotto and we know the numbers in advance.

Evenings were the best time. I preferred to take Charmaine out to dinner. She usually wanted to cook for me. Playing house agreed with her. She didn't have much to learn from those actresses she was so fond of watching. Her charm was natural; it oozed from every pore of her body. I discovered that she liked reading those old comic books I had bought from Tommy, especially *Superman.* "Charmaine, haven't you ever read comics before?"

"My grandpa wouldn't buy such things. I only saw them in the Sunday paper or when we went into town. When my sister and I were growing up, our biggest thrill was going into town to see a movie. We always had the radio shows, you know. Grandma and Grandpa liked the Lum and Abner and Burns and Allen. For my sister and me, the Shadow was our favorite."

Leaving home and becoming part of the modern world would have made Charmaine an adventuress in the 1940s. But even though this girl didn't know it, she was pretty conservative. Growing up on a farm in Wisconsin, she had spent most of her Wednesday evenings and Sunday mornings at the Lutheran Church. And the three room school house where she went through all of her grades wasn't exactly Berkeley in the '60s.

chapter

7

Under the Looking Glass

I couldn't sleep very long. Excitement filled me knowing I would soon be off this cruiser and back on land. I went out on deck and headed for the bow. Soon I was lost in thought as I marveled how things could work out this way. Incredible! Just over three months ago I was in Laguna, California in 2007. I emerged in 1944 and met Charmaine. Now fate would bring me to Darwin, Australia in 1945. When did my dream start to fall apart? Oh yes, I was on the run, I remember now. My activities were under the looking glass and I realized it too late.

———

The treasury man waited impatiently in the reception room of the FBI Field Headquarters in Los Angeles. The receptionist had just put in a call on the intercom to the director,

Mr. Cadwell. The director's door opened and he came out personally to meet the treasury man. Cadwell walked up to him, offered his hand. Mr. Arnstadt?

"Yes," replied the thin man wearing glasses, nervously.

"A pleasure to make your acquaintance. Please come into my office."

They walked inside and Cadwell motioned for him to take a seat. "I received a rather urgent call from J. Edgar this morning to give you the utmost cooperation. It seems whatever your business is, it won't wait. I understand you just flew in from Washington. Now, can you tell me what this is all about?"

Arnstadt opened his briefcase and pulled out a manila envelope. He opened it and took out an assortment of paper money. He set them on the desk, took the top one, and handed it to Cadwell. "Please look at this twenty, sir; tell me what you think?"

Cadwell took the twenty dollar bill; thumbed it, turned it around and around and handed it back to Arnstadt. "Don't worry, we'll pick this genius up straightaway. Imagine putting the date 1945 on a counterfeit bill in 1944."

Arnstadt declined to take it back. "Look at it again, sir; tell me what else you think."

Cadwell looked at it more closely as he turned it over and over. "Sure, it looks good. How does that change anything?"

"Mr. Cadwell, it is perfect in every detail. Our lab determined that the ink and paper are authentic. Do you realize how difficult it would be to replicate the ink? Someone would have to have access to the secret formula. And we've checked the paper source at the plant in Connecticut. It is rigidly controlled there and no losses can be accounted for. This stuff looked so good;

we checked and verified that these serial numbers had not been issued yet."

Cadwell contemplated as he stared at the stack of bills. He rubbed his chin as he spoke. "Why would anyone who is capable of producing anything as good as this be so stupid as to place a future date on it?" he asked casually.

"That's not all, Mr. Cadwell; you'll see it also has the appearance of being aged."

Cadwell shrugged as he felt the texture of the twenty between his fingers. "Again, Mr. Arnstadt, why would anyone who could produce this kind of work feel the need to do such a thing?"

"I don't know, Mr. Cadwell; but we are at war. Our immediate concern is that the Axis forces, particularly the Germans, may be trying to flood our country with this bogus money and undermine our economy. They have already tried that in Europe with the British five pound note."

"What about those other bills, Mr. Arnstadt?"

"Here, look at them. There are fives, tens and even ones here." He shoved the small stack toward Cadwell. "Whoever is doing this is reproducing money of all denominations. And look; they all have different serial numbers, even the ones. Whoever is doing this has an unlimited range of ability. They're not limited to using one plate. Can you imagine what will happen to us when this stuff starts flooding the country? The entire U.S. economy is at risk of being destroyed. Also, each of these bills is in a different stage of the aging process. Look at these two twenties. One of them has had more exposure to light. It would normally take dozens of years to produce that effect."

Cadwell furrowed his brow as he continued to gaze at them. "Why would anyone age a bill that is supposed to be brand new? It would be counter productive. This is perplexing, Mr. Arnstadt. The only thing I can imagine is that maybe the local agent sprung this stuff in advance of his instructions. Perhaps this foreign agent turned renegade, and is serving his own needs. It is pretty clear by now that Germany is going to lose this war."

"The story is even stranger than that, Mr. Cadwell. Here is the background. Two weeks ago, our office in Washington received a call from the reserve bank out here. This was our first notice of these bills. These had almost passed unnoticed at the local banks; and they would have except for the vigilance of a local teller here in Los Angeles. Well, as you can imagine, we started investigating immediately. We determined that some of the money was deposited from two sources. One was from a pawn broker in downtown L.A. The other strangely enough, came from a ten year old boy in Burbank."

"We need to interrogate them immediately," replied Cadwell. "These must be the people we were instructed to bring in this morning. They are in the hallway right now."

"I know, Mr. Cadwell. I arranged that myself through your Division Headquarters in San Francisco. They passed those instructions on to you. Our treasury agents here questioned them before your people picked them up. For the most part, they seem cooperative. One of them is a ten year old boy named Tommy Thompson. It seems a man accompanied by a young blonde woman might have paid him twenty dollars for a *Superman* comic book three weeks ago, on a Monday. The owner of the little store in Burbank remembered that Tommy bought some things that day, and paid with a twenty dollar bill. When the store owner attempted to make a deposit, the teller at the bank noticed the date on the bill. He excused himself and reported it to the bank president, who in turn called the police. The store owner was taken in for questioning. He said it might have come from the boy, but he wasn't sure. Tommy was brought in for questioning. A check of the fingerprints on the bill proved that he did actually handle it. We are trying to identify the other prints now, but so far without any luck."

"How about his parents?"

"The police gave them a clean bill, Mr. Cadwell. His mother is a housewife with five children still at home. Their oldest son is in the Navy. The dad works at a defense plant in Burbank."

"And the other individual, Mr. Arnstadt?"

"He's a pawn broker in downtown L.A. by the name of Mark Cohen. We traced some bills to him by his fingerprints which were already on file. He may be our best lead. He has been on the police watch list for a long time for possibly being a receiver of stolen goods."

Cadwell pushed the button on his intercom. "Miss McDaniel, please have those folks waiting in the hallway come into my office." It was less than a minute before Miss McDaniel opened the door and walked in. She was followed by four people. Little Tommy Thompson came in first with his mother and father. Mark Cohen followed closely behind. After introductions, Cadwell asked Cohen to wait in the lobby and then he proceeded to question Tommy.

"Tommy, do you know why you're here today?"

The boy nervously answered, "Because I took twenty dollars from a man? I never copt it; honest! He wanted to buy my old comic book. He gave me twenty dollars for it." Tommy appeared on the verge of tears and his parents looked worried.

"You want me to believe that this man paid you twenty dollars for a comic book?"

"It's true; I ain't lying. You gotta believe me." Tommy slowly started sobbing.

Cadwell could see that he was telling the truth. The boy was scared but he was not a liar. "Easy, Tommy; nobody is accusing you of anything. We just want to know why a man would do such a thing."

Tommy's father tried to shield his son. "There's no crime in selling comic books, Mr. Cadwell."

"I didn't say there was, Mr. Thompson; but we have a deeper mystery here. And I must ask you to remain quiet or I'll have you removed from the room. Do you understand?"

"Yes, sir!"

"Now, Tommy, do you know this man? What did he look like?"

"I never seen him before then, sir. He wore a dark suit and had a hat and tie. And the lady called him John."

"John? Did you hear any more names; what about hers?"

"I don't remember any. Oh yeah, he called her honey! He looked older than her."

"How did you meet them, Tommy?" "I was playin' baseball with Russell and the other boys on Sunday afternoon. Russ told me there was this guy, and he wanted to buy comic books and baseball cards. Russell is a paper boy and he sees a lots of guys."

"And then what did you say?"

"Well, I asked him if I could meet the guy too. He said sure! I'll be hangin' around the corner market off Victory just like most days sellin' papers. If I see him; I'll tell you."

"And then what happened?"

"I was home Monday afternoon, and Russ come to see me. He told me the man who wanted the comics was gonna be at the market in a little while. So I showed up with a armful of old comics. They used to belong to my older brother Billy. He's in the Navy. But he give 'em to me before he went away."

"And then?"

"This man and lady came in a car. We was standin' there and Russ said, 'That's him.'"

"What kind of a car was it, Tommy?"

"A DeSoto."

"Color?"

"Brown."

"What year?"

"38 I think, sir."

"I don't suppose you remember the plate?"

"Naw!"

"What then, Tommy?"

"And then he come up to us and said hi to me and Russ. Then Russ told me to show him my old comic books."

"Go on, Tommy; you're doing fine."

"Well, he looked at my stack of comics; and when he found *Superman*, he asked me how much I wanted for it."

"Your answer?"

"I said twenty-five cents. And then he pulled out twenty dollars and gave it to me."

Cadwell paused and turned to Arnstadt. "Did your people corroborate this with the other boy? Arnstadt nodded.

"Did they say where they were from, Tommy?"

"No, sir."

Cadwell asked him a few more questions before telling the Thompsons they could leave.

After they were gone, Arnstadt said, "Mr. Cohen's story is even stranger; but it backs up little Tommy's statement."

"We'll see," replied Cadwell. Then he called Miss McDaniel over the intercom. "Miss McDaniel, please send in Mr. Cohen."

Cohen walked in and Cadwell motioned him to a chair. "Well, Mr. Cohen, we would like to ask you a few questions."

Cohen was surly. "Can I have my lawyer present?"

"Mr. Cohen, you had better cooperate without hesitation," said Cadwell. "We can bury you in a pit so deep that sunshine couldn't even be pumped in to you. Understand?"

The bluff worked; Cohen was visibly shaken. "Yes, sir."

Indeed, Cohen's statements were as perplexing as Tommy's had been. Cohen went on to describe how this well dressed man named John Moses with his blonde companion came into his shop on a Monday. He described how this man was asking about coins, baseball cards and other collectibles. Cohen admitted that he had charged outrageous prices for some coins which the man paid without even a question. Cohen's information was more detailed. He admitted that he asked the man to check back in about a week. But the man hadn't returned. Cadwell interrogated Cohen extensively before he allowed him to leave.

After Cohen was gone, Cadwell and Arnstadt reviewed both stories. Both thought Levi would be the best lead. "We'll watch this one," said Cadwell. "I'll also have a stakeout placed on that little market in Burbank. Our people will search the files in Washington for anything fitting this individual named John Moses. We'll compare these fingerprints with those already in our data base. And, we'll bring in these witnesses again so they can give more physical details of this man and woman. Our forensic artists are very proficient at reproducing good likenesses from these descriptions."

Miles away from the FBI Office, Lander took Charmaine's hand and pressed it to his lips as they snuggled in bed in their new Glendale apartment.

"Honey, let's get dressed. We're going away for a couple of days."

"Everyday with you is a vacation, Johnny. It's never dull. I suppose I better ask where we're going?"

"Las Vegas, my pretty squeeze!"

She scowled at me. "I don't think I like being called a squeeze; it sounds like another name for a broad." Then her tone became slightly more agreeable. "Why would anyone want to go there anyway?"

"We're going on a shopping trip, sweetie."

Immediately Charmaine became enthusiastic as she raised her eyebrows. "You always get these strange ideas, Johnny. What kind of shopping are you going to do there?"

"Coins, Charmaine honey; more coins, just like always! Coins with a Carson City mint mark! I haven't found many around here that I really want. And the ones I did aren't particularly valuable to me. There may be some in a private collection there in Nevada, and Las Vegas is the closest place to us from here. Besides, we'll have another chance to play in the sun. You don't know it, but that will be big city of well over two million people some day."

"How could you possibly know such a thing, Johnny? Who would build a city that big over there? I think I passed through there coming to California on the train. Isn't it just desert?"

"That's a fact, lady. That is a fact! But Nevada is the only state at the moment that allows legalized gambling. And it will remain that way for a long time. After the war, the smart cookies, especially the mob people, are going to build casinos there. Las Vegas will become a Mecca for entertainment. People will come from the East Coast, even Europe and Asia to gamble and play there."

She looked at me skeptically. "That's a long way to drive, Johnny."

"No, honey, we're going by train. I don't trust the DeSoto, even with its new tires for this one." Another idea began to develop in my mind. I couldn't buy any property in this here and now. But Charmaine could. Did I dare use her as a surrogate for my ambitions? How deep did I want to get involved with her anyway? I mulled these thoughts around and around as we went to Union Terminal later that day. I left a few thousand dollars at the apartment and placed fifty more in the glove compartment as a precaution. After she parked the car, we walked inside the station lobby into the midst of hundreds of uniformed men and civilians going everywhere. I had never imagined that Union Station could look like this. Trains were on every track. I didn't see how they could move about. Steam from the long black locomotives was everywhere. I bought two round trip tickets to Las Vegas and we boarded late that afternoon on a Santa Fe passenger train bound for Vegas.

We experienced some delays in sidings while meeting other passenger trains, especially troop trains. We finally stepped off the train at 4:10 A.M. the next morning in the Union Pacific Las Vegas Station. I took Charmaine by the hand. From there it was a short walk to the Golden Gate Casino. This place I recognized. I was fortunate to get us a room there and registered us under the name of Mr. and Mrs. Kirk. Charmaine took notice but didn't question me about it. We went upstairs and wasted no time going to bed. I was up by nine. She was still tired from the trip and I let her sleep the rest of the morning.

Outside, I strolled down Fremont. So this is what it looked like. I walked around and recognized the El Cortez. A landmark, the Pioneer was there, but without the waving cowboy. I walked into the Apache which I knew in later times as the Horseshoe and went to the bar.

"What can I get for you?" asked the aged bartender pleasantly.

"Can I just get a cup of Joe?"

"Sure," he replied and quickly brought me a cup.

I laid some money on the bar.

"Forget it," he said. We always try to sober up the drunks before they leave; the boss man likes it that way. Where from stranger?"

"At the moment, Glendale, California. John Kirk is my name. What's yours?"

"Fred," he replied as we shook hands. The bar wasn't very busy yet and we were able to talk for a while. Fred was from Chicago, and had come out west after his doctor had suggested that he move to a dry climate.

He brought me a second cup of coffee before I turned to business. "Fred, are any of your customers here local folks?"

"Sure, lots! Why?"

"Well, I'm looking to do some buying locally. I'm interested in Nevada artifacts. Do you know anybody that I could hook up with on this?"

"It's your lucky day; just a minute." He walked to the other end of the bar and talked to an old-timer in shabby clothes with a long, unkempt beard and a slouch hat. Fred pointed toward me.

The old-timer rose up and ambled casually toward me. He came face to face as he somberly looked at me. "Howdy mister!"

"Howdy yourself," I replied. "Join me; I'll buy you a drink." I motioned to the stool next to me and waved to Fred. He shoved it aside and leaned against the bar, just like he had at the other end.

Fred came up to him. "Shot of rye here, Fred."

"Coming up, Sam."

"You got business of sorts here in town, mister?"

"Yes. I'm a collector and I have something specific in mind. Did I hear him call you, Sam?"

"You did!" It turned out Sam was a prospector. He participated in the Alaska gold rush when he was still in his teens, and had followed this pursuit all over the west ever since. His sun baked, crinkled skin was darker than a walnut; and with one look at him, it was clear he was on hard times. When that first shot of rye went down with a single gulp, I knew we were going to be here for a while.

"Hey, Fred, set Sam up again!"

Several drinks and many old stories later, old Sam became almost amiable. "What are you a collectin' stranger?" he asked. Sam never did get around to asking me my name.

"I'm interested in Nevada history, including the gold and silver mining. And I'm particularly interested in the old mint at Carson City. I would like to increase my collection of coins minted there. Do you know anybody that could help me?"

"Could be," he replied.

Old Sam could be very laconic when he wasn't telling his old stories. I knew I would have to continue priming his pump and ordered him another rye. Fred returned with the drink and then got busy elsewhere.

Old Sam finally came around to the subject. "There's an old gal, lives a few blocks from here, a retired school teacher. Peculiar old gal, she never got married. I used to come into town and run into her once in a while. She knew I was a miner and always asked me if I had anything to show her. Ever once in a while she'd buy some dust from me and also asked if she could see my coins. I let her go through my change and sometimes she wanted to buy a coin or two from me. I heard she also sometimes bought the coins put in the offering plate at her church after the service. Funny old gal!"

"Is she still alive, Sam?"

"Don't know!"

"Sam, if you take me to her, the drinks are on me the rest of the day."

"All right, let's do it, mister." Sam took me to a small house on a side street not far away. He pointed to it and told me her name was Edna Van Fleet. It was almost noon and I knew I shouldn't neglect Charmaine any longer. I thanked him and gave him a twenty dollar bill. Sam was overjoyed to get it. We walked back toward Fremont Street together. At the door of the Apache, he wished me good luck, and we parted company. He turned and walked inside. I kept going to the Golden Gate at the end of Fremont. I went up the stairs and opened the door to our room.

Charmaine was laying in her slip on the bed, smoking and listening to the radio. "What are you listening to, baby?"

"More war news, honey. I hope the boys can come home someday soon, like you said they would. Where have you been, Johnny?"

"Prospecting, sweetie!"

She gave me an 'oh really' look. "We came all the way here to go shopping and now you're prospecting. I couldn't begin to understand you in two life times, Johnny."

I smiled. "No one has called me Johnny this much since I was a boy. I like it, sweetie! Anyway, prospecting is just a figure of speech, baby. Get your shoes on and I'll get you something to eat, but first I want to meet a lady before it gets too late."

"Meet a lady?"

"Retired school teacher, honey! She may have something I need."

"I've never met anyone in my life who needs expensive old coins. You always have money, but I wonder what you really do for a living."

I ran my fingers through her pretty blond hair and gently pulled her to me. Then I kissed her on the tip of her nose. She smiled with pleasure. "I'm really a magician, sweetie; I make things happen that weren't meant to."

Soon we were slowly strolling with our arms around each other toward Edna Van Fleet's house. I knocked several times until a plump white haired lady in a faded polka dot dress answered the door.

"May I help you?" she asked pleasantly.

"Yes, mam. I'm a collector of Nevada artifacts, and your name was mentioned as a possible source. Can I discuss the matter with you further?"

"Do you mean that I should sell some to you? I don't think so, but please come in and have some tea, and I'll show you some of my collection. What are your names?"

"John Kirk and my lady friend, Charmaine," I replied.

She shook hands with us and we were led into her tidy parlor. Miss Van Fleet asked us to sit down. Charmaine commented on all of her nice, pretty collectibles and Miss Van Fleet began to warm up to us. She excused herself and went into her kitchen. Soon, she had a pot of hot tea brewing and it wasn't long before she returned with a tray. "I don't have any lemons. But would either of you like some sugar?" Charmaine took some and we sipped our tea.

"What kind of artifacts are you interested in, Mr. Kirk?"

"Things unique to Nevada history," I replied.

"Well, I wish I could have had this kind of interest out of my students when I was still teaching." She excused herself and returned soon with some boxes which turned out to be Piute Indian Artifacts.

"Actually, Miss Van Fleet, I am more interested in Nevada's mining history; the old mint at Carson City, that sort of thing you see."

"Please call me Edna. I do have some old coins; would you like to see them?"

"Very much so, Edna! Thank you."

Again she got up and returned with another box. She took them out one by one and began telling personal stories about them. I could tell that this lonely, old lady was enjoying sharing her collection with us. I looked at them one by one until I sat stunned. I was holding an 1873 CC dime in mint perfect condition. One of these had sold for over $600,000 back in 1999.

Many others in her possession would be worth thousands in my time. I gave it back to her expressing my desire to buy if she was willing to part with it.

She smiled, "These are becoming quite rare, Mr. Kirk. I've had this since I was a very young woman. I wouldn't want to part with it."

"I'll pay you five hundred dollars, mam."

It was her turn to be stunned. "Why do you want it that much, Mr. Kirk?"

"I'm a collector, mam; it will complete my set of Carson City dimes. And frankly, I haven't been able to find one with this date anywhere."

Edna sat there reflecting before replying. "I really don't have anyone to leave them to. I had a niece in Ely, but she passed on years ago and her children never write me. This is tempting Mr. Kirk; the money would be useful." She reflected for several moments. "Yes, Mr. Kirk, I will sell it to you at that price."

She allowed me to purchase a few more coins, and I gave her an even thousand dollars in the transaction. Then she wanted to show me old newspapers she had saved. I knew there was money to be made there too, but I told her another time. As we departed down the street she watched and waved. I took Charmaine by the hand as we walked. I was feeling lucky.

Charmaine was silent and seemed lost in thought for several minutes. "How much money did you get from that, Johnny?" she finally asked.

"Oh, about a dollar and a half in face value, honey. Why?"

"You're a madman. I've got it figured out; you're a madman. You escaped from a lunatic asylum and I met you. Then I fell in love with a madman."

I stopped and gently swung her around as I looked into her eyes. "You love me?" In all of our brief time together, though we had both felt it, neither of us had ever used the word love before.

"Yes, and I must be as crazy as you are. What do you do for a living that you can buy little things for this kind of money? You seem to have plenty of money. But none of this makes any sense to me."

This became the defining moment in out relationship. "Charmaine?"

"Yes, Johnny!"

"Are you along for the ride; I can make it a good one?"

"Oh, you know I am. Do you love me too?"

"More than anything! If nothing else good came out of this, it was worth coming back here just for you."

She furrowed her brow. "Coming back here, what do you mean by that?"

"It doesn't mean anything, honey; just forget it. I know you're hungry. Aren't you?"

"No, I'm starving!"

We made our way to the Apache. Old Sam was pretty animated and quite jovial. He invited us to join him for a drink at the bar.

"Thanks, another time, Sam," I said. I took Charmaine into the diner. I was confident, riding high with the sweet smell of success. Hank would be pleased. The red wine and steak were especially good. Charmaine wasn't much of a drinker. She wanted milk at least three times a day. After our meal I felt like having fun. "Hey, let's pop over to the El Cortes for a quick drink, a celebration. Besides I want to see what it looks like in these times"

Charmaine leaned against me as we walked along. "Johnny, how could anyone celebrate trading a thousand dollars for a little over one dollar in old coins? Oh, I'm with you, honey. Sure, let's get a drink." She looked up at me with puzzled expression. "Did you come from Mars or something?"

"Maybe I did! Still love me?"

She smiled. "Yes. Johnny, why do you always say, these times?"

"Ha, ha, ha! Don't think twice about it when I say that, honey. I only meant the war, what else?" We walked into the bar of the El Cortez. Fred, the bartender from the Apache was there. He was having an off duty drink with a lady friend. We exchanged pleasantries and I introduced him to Charmaine. I ordered bourbon on the rocks; she wanted a Tom Collins.

I saw a blackjack dealer sitting alone. Maybe I could pick up some easy money. I read Thorpe's book on blackjack strategy many years ago. It was published well after the war. These people shouldn't be aware of card counting techniques. That wasn't exactly so as I would find out. I decided to play a few hands while Charmaine drifted about playing the slots. Things went well at first. I increased my bet when the count turned favorable and won a few easy hands. The pit boss was watching me steadily, and then the dealer was switched out. That should have been my cue to get out, but I was flush with confidence. The cocktail waitress never let my glass stay empty. We were playing single deck blackjack. This new dealer had the ultimate poker face as he watched my play. My luck started to go south and so did my cash. Then the count became really favorable. The deck was rich in face cards and I bet half of my cash. I was dealt an eleven. Using the rest of my money, I doubled down. The dealer had a six showing, the worst possible card. I felt confident. This was the real Lander; put it on the line and take a chance. The dealer turned up a two for my hand making thirteen. Then he revealed his hand. He had an ace in the hole, seventeen. I was wiped out.

His face never showed any emotion as he looked at me. "You seem to be out of chips, sir. Looks like you've had your share of fun. Anything else I can do for you?"

I suspected things weren't on the up and up, but didn't argue with him. I walked over to the bar and spoke to Fred. "Fred, do you see that dealer over there?"

He didn't wait for me to say another word. "That guy is a card mechanic with mob connections," he said under his breath. "He and the pit boss were talking about you earlier. Buddy, you had better get out; they didn't like your play."

I nodded and took his advice. Drawing attention was something I couldn't risk. I found Charmaine and we left. As we walked along Fremont Street, I felt like a fool. There was no reason to remain in Las Vegas any longer. We were broke but at least I'd had enough sense to buy round trip tickets and prepay our room. We walked to the Union Pacific Station where I checked the schedules. We could leave town at 3:15 A.M.

"What are we going to do now, Johnny?"

"Let's get some sleep; we'll leave early in the morning," I replied.

At the hotel, I asked the desk clerk to give us a wake up call at 1:30 A.M. We had a chance for a few hours sleep and before long were between the sheets. We quickly snuggled together in a warm embrace. Calling it an early evening did have its rewards!

One thirty came quickly. We packed our things into the suitcase and checked out. If the train was on time we should have been in L.A. around noon. As luck would have it, this was not the case. There had been a derailment east of Las Vegas. It would be an indefinite period of time before we could board and leave town. At ten o'clock that morning Charmaine was visibly uncomfortable with hunger. It was gnawing at my stomach too. A full eighteen hours had passed since our last meal. "Do you have any money, Charmaine?"

"No, I put all of mine into the slot machines. But you still have plenty of money, don't you, Johnny?"

I reached down in my pocket and pulled out all of my loose change. All I had was seven cents. I pulled out my wallet and took out those few coins I had bought from Mrs. Van Fleet. Examining them, I tucked the 1873 CC dime back into a niche in my wallet and looked at the rest. Well, life has strange twists, I thought. "Come on, sweetie; these coins in my hand tell me you're going to get something to eat."

"But they cost you hundreds of dollars. How can you?"

"It's OK, Charmaine; I know how to replace them. Just a minor inconvenience! Let's just think of ourselves as millionaires who don't care a whit how much things cost."

"You already act like a millionaire, Johnny! I never understood the meaning of eccentric until I met you."

"I'll buy you something to eat, baby. I can go without."

"Johnny, if you don't eat, I don't eat!"

"You drive a hard bargain, pretty one." I ran my fingers through her golden hair and pulled her into me. "OK, come on!" We went back to the Golden Gate and each of us had ham and eggs with coffee. It only cost me thirty cents for each of us.

So, I was able to save some more of my new toys. I didn't tip this time, even though this wasn't my style. We were able to board our train a few minutes after noon. Owing to the delays caused by that derailment, we didn't arrive in L.A. until 11:00 that night.

———

Christmas 1944, was the best I ever had. Charmaine originally planned for us to go to her sister's house for Christmas Eve dinner. We had been invited. But that plan fell apart when her brother-in-law, Tom, found out we were living together. By the standards of these times, that made us unacceptable in respectable circles. This was a secret relief to me. He would have only asked me a lot of uncomfortable questions about myself. At first, Charmaine sheepishly tried to break the news to me. She had been told she was welcome, but that I couldn't go.

"John, honey, I told my sister that I wouldn't go without you. But I'm going to go by there Christmas Day with some presents for my niece and nephew."

"No problem with me, sweetie; what's up anyway?"

"Tom doesn't like that we're living together. He says it's a bad influence on his kids."

"Hells bells, are they old enough to even know or care?"

Charmaine giggled. "No, it's Tom himself, and my sister too!"

"Is Tom an old man?"

"No. He is about twenty-five, a year older than my sister; I think."

"How come he's not in the service?"

"He has some kind of job deferment. A railroad worker, you know, at some place called Taylor Yard over by Atwater. Back in Wisconsin his family was very stuffy too."

"Punish me, Tom!" I yelled loudly. "Who the hell wants to see you anyway!"

Charmaine burst out laughing. "Johnny, how much do you love me?"

"More than I thought a man could love, honey."

"When did you first start loving me?"

"Probably before I ever knew you; every man longs for his own Charmaine."

"How do I know that you love me, Johnny?" she teased.

I pulled her gently into my arms. "The curtain just went up for us, and it's going to be a long play."

She smothered my mouth with kisses. "Will you always love me?"

"I'm not sure, sweetie; always is a long time. Some day I'm going to die, but it looks like a pretty good bet till then. And beyond that, if possible, yes!"

"Oh, Johnny, shut up. You're always a smart aleck. You better take me quick before I force myself on you first."

"You can't force the willing! Besides, imagine that, I got first place over Christmas dinner with Tom!"

"Oh, Johnny! I'd rather eat hot dogs with you than have steak with anyone else." I scooped her into my arms and laid her gently on the bed. She ran her fingers through my hair. "Johnny, you have such warm brown eyes but your hair is getting thin on top."

"What do you think I am, baby, just another pretty face?"

She giggled. "Now, John, now!

Later that evening, we snuggled as I drew her into my arms. "Charmaine honey, remind me to send a thank you card to Tom."

She rolled over and kissed both of my eyes. "My papa used to kiss my eyes this way after I went to bed. Hush, Johnny, go to sleep!"

———

We were in the last week of December. It had been fun! Six weeks that seemed like paradise compared to the 21st century. Sure, I missed my computer, driving my modern car and all of the electronic conveniences I was used to. But this had been time out of anything I had ever known. The feel of life was different. California was a paradise in the 1940s and none of the people of these times knew it. It was taken for granted. The only social issues were submerged with the preoccupation of winning the war. People still had time to have fun, to love, and there was no shortage of work. The doom and gloom for the future, that I was so used to in my own time, didn't exist here. There was only unbounded optimism, and no two hours spent on some lousy freeway either. That nagging thought crept back into my mind again; I could live here real easy.

I carefully laid out all of the coins and collectibles on the bed, and made some mental calculations. I estimated its worth at seven million, and still an easy three and a half we heavily discounted it. If only I had arrived as originally planned and got those bets in. This would amount to a couple hundred million. It didn't occur to me that I wouldn't have met Charmaine if everything had worked out as planned. I'll return to my own time. Hank and I will sell these goods. We'll buy more old money, and I'll come back for the big kill.

We'll have to calibrate the machine better than the first time. I toyed with the idea of making this unsophisticated era my playground. This was too good to be true. We could buy one hundred times as much old money, and then increase it one hundredfold. Meet John Lander, the world's newest billionaire. Move over Bill Gates. You finally made it big, John Lander!

Suddenly, I became worried. This wasn't the first time this nagging thought came into my mind. Old Hank might not want me to come back again. He only wanted enough money to finance his way into his future, whatever the hell that might be. Suppose he tries to stop me from coming back? Well, he needs me as much as I need him. We'll just work that out when I decide to return.

I packed all of the collectibles together in my two grips. Charmaine stood there watching me pensively. I would miss her, even if it was only for a few days. Wait, I thought. It might seem like a few days to me, but I'll fine tune the machine. It may be only hours or even minutes here. She was going to be safely tucked away in the apartment and well provided for. There was still almost two months rent left on the books, and I gave her an extra two hundred dollars. While the words were unsaid, it was clear we would stay together. Our future relationship was vague. I took her for granted, putting out of my mind the fact that I unalterably changed her future, and possibly that of many others. But, Charmaine baby, you're going to remain mine. What would Hank say about her? He wouldn't approve! He wouldn't have to! I won't tell him.

"I'll be gone for a while, honey; buy yourself something pretty. With this, and the other money I gave you, it will keep you going nicely till I get back."

"Can't I go too, Johnny?"

"Not this time, lady; but I'll be back soon enough. I need you here. We have to keep this apartment, and you have to keep on checking out leads of those things I want."

"Can't you at least tell me where you're going?"

"Uh, uh, but I have buyers waiting for these goods."

"People really buy this stuff, Johnny?"

"Oh, Charmaine, if you only knew!"

"Why can't you tell me? You're always so mysterious about everything. Why don't you let me drive you to the station?"

"I've got a taxi waiting outside, honey; let's leave it at that." We walked to the front door of the apartment. Once there I kissed her long and deep. Her eyes began to mist. I couldn't let this affect me. I turned away.

Walking out of the apartment, I felt lucky. I walked down the hallway and out through the security door. The taxi was waiting by the curb in front of the apartment building. I waved to the driver who nodded for me to get in. "Hello," I said as I placed my grips in the back seat.

"Do you want to put those in the trunk?" returned the Cabbie.

"No, thanks; I'll be getting out soon enough. Take me to the San Fernando Valley along Victory Blvd. Turn right on Topanga Canyon Road when you get to Canoga Park. I'll tell you where to turn from there."

"That's quite a ways. You could probably take the red car and get pretty close to where you're goin', mister."

"No, I'm going to Chatsworth; the red car doesn't reach that far. And I'd rather go by taxi anyway."

"I'm your man; where to exactly?"

"It'll be easier if I just direct you. I'll tell you where to turn when I see it."

"Well OK," said the cabbie.

We exchanged pleasantries during the drive. The cab driver was a horse player, and that subject always gained my attention. As we approached the gas station I said to him, "Turn here." Within minutes we would be at the crossroads by the orange groves. I needed to stop the cab before reaching them. I couldn't risk being spotted from the Woodward place.

"Please stop here, driver; I feel like walking."

"Why? I'll just take you all the way."

"I was raised around here. I want to look the place over."

"Are you sure, mister? I'd rather drive you."

"I want to walk. Please stop now." He almost started to argue, and then stopped. I decided to give him a little something extra. I gave him a twenty and told him to keep the change. I felt generous; after all, I was going to be enormously rich soon. That was a week's wages to him.

He took it with eyes wide open. "Gee, thanks!"

"Oh, one more thing, buddy," I said before closing the door. "They're going to allow the track at Santa Anita to open up this spring. I heard from a good source that Busher is going to be the horse of the year in 1945 and the best filly."

He waved me off with his right hand, and shook his head. "I never bet on fillies."

"Well," I said, "You know what works for you."

The cab driver made a u-turn. I slowly started walking down the dirt road by the grove. Then, I swung inside the orchard as soon as the cab was gone. I quickly reached the recall point. Looking at my watch, I waited patiently for the appointed hour. I turned on the beacon one minute before recall. When the time came, nothing happened. Three hours later I was in a state of anxiety and semi-desperation. What went wrong? The Einstein-Rosen Bridge had been set to open exactly six weeks after I landed in this time. And then I realized what the problem must be. This wasn't early June. I had landed five months too early. The synchronization for the wormhole was imperfect. There's no telling when it's going to open. But, it should open next June, as we intended. My only hope was to survive until then. I decided to make my way back to Charmaine.

It was a forty minute ride. I slid out of the passenger's seat of the old '37 Chevy pickup and offered the farmer some money. "Thanks for bringing me all the way into Burbank, sir. I know you were only going into Van Nuys."

But he wouldn't take it. "I saw your ring, mister. I wouldn't charge anybody for a ride, but for a fellow Mason I would go that extra mile."

We said our goodbyes. There was a phone booth on the corner by a drug store. I went over to it, took both valises with me inside and closed the door.

I put my nickel in, dialed '0' and waited for the operator. "Number please?" she asked.

Very soon the phone in our apartment stopped ringing and I heard Charmaine's voice. "Hello?"

"Honey, I'll be with you soon. I had some trouble and can't leave town for a while."

"Johnny, what have you done?"

"Done? What do you mean, Charmaine baby?"

"I went by my old apartment in Burbank to check on my mail. Mrs. Landry told me the FBI had been in the neighborhood looking for a man named John Moses who had been seen at the market on Victory."

"Did she tell you why they wanted him, Charmaine?"

"She said they were looking for the man passing counterfeit currency, the notes with 1945 dates on them."

Oh God! How could I be so stupid? I had planned to come back to May of 1945. But I landed in November of 1944. Some of the old notes we bought were from 1945. What was I going to do? I don't exist on paper; I couldn't allow myself to be taken. "Honey, I wasn't passing counterfeit notes. This is going to be really hard to explain. Please trust me?"

"I never doubted you for a moment, Johnny. I don't care what they say."

"Charmaine, did Mrs. Landry say anything about a woman being seen with the man?"

"Yes, Johnny, a blonde woman."

"This is worse than I thought. Was she suspicious of you?"

"I don't think so. She just acted like her usual self."

"Look, Charmaine; listen carefully. I'm going to have to lie low for awhile, disappear. We have to separate for a short time; we can't be seen together."

"Why can't we just go away together, Johnny?"

"Because the FBI and cops are going to be looking for a man in his thirties traveling with a young blonde woman. Too many people have seen us together. You've got to get out of that apartment in Glendale. Destroy anything that I left behind. And before you leave, wipe every hard surface clean with bleach. Even the walls! No fingerprints, yours or mine, understand? Tell the landlord that I had a job offer in San Francisco, one that I can't pass up. Tell him I went there already, and we don't care about the overpayment of rent. We won't take any chances." Suddenly, I thought about the DeSoto. Fortunately, we had forgotten to register it. "Charmaine honey, wipe the inside of the DeSoto clean of prints too, the handles, steering wheel, and dashboard, anything with a hard surface. Use bleach. Burn the pink slip, and leave it parked on a side street with the keys in it over in East L.A. OK?"

"Yes, Johnny!"

"And, Charmaine, don't go back to Burbank!"

"Johnny, can't you tell me what this is all about?"

"Honey, I haven't done anything wrong. But there is something that these people wouldn't understand. I won't contact you for a while, maybe even for a few months. Wherever you go, make sure your sister knows where I can find you. Make sure she promises to give me your address. O.K.?"

"Yes, but I don't want to lose you, Johnny."

"You won't lose me, Charmaine. Look, I love you. But this mess is bigger than you can imagine. I might even explain it to you someday. Or maybe I won't. I have to get away and think things out. And if this gets totally out of control, I don't want you to be a part of it. Understand?"

"No!"

"But you'll do what I say?"

"Yes, Johnny!"

"Before I forget, what is your sister's address and phone number?"

"Her name is Barbara Swenson. She lives at 354 Elm in Canoga Park and her phone number is State 642."

"Honey, let me write that down. I won't try to call you until I know it is safe. They may tap your phone. Don't make any more calls from the apartment. If I can, I'll send some money to you through your sister."

"This isn't goodbye forever is it, Johnny?

"No, nothing like that! Have faith in me, honey. O.K.?"

"O.K., Johnny!"

"I've got to go now, Charmaine. I can't tell you where I'm going. But I'll come back to you. Just do what I said, and tell your sister to let me know how to find you. Tell me you'll do this!"

Sounds of sobbing were flowing over the line. "O.K., Johnny, I love you; I don't want to lose you."

"Goodbye, Charmaine. I love you too; goodbye." I hung up the phone. Well if I go down, I'm going down alone. I have to protect her. But for now, I must hide.

Hank noted with satisfaction the departure of Lander. He recorded the details in his ledger before getting up. "I'll take a fifteen minute break, get a cup of coffee, and then bring him back."

Hank finished microwaving a cup of old coffee and sipped it as he walked back to the workshop. Taking his time, he sat down at the control station and advanced the machine's settings in 1945 for the recall time. Our moment of truth, Hank thought! I wonder what John will bring back. Well, this is the wavelength that should bring him back six weeks later in 1945. Hank's confidence was high. Together, the two had experimented with this timing sequence by sending back an atomic clock. They monitored its departure and return by measuring its changes against various wavelengths. It worked fine on those few tests. But too much had been taken for granted.

Hank partially opened the bridge, and waited patiently for the recall signal from Lander's beacon. Nothing happened. He fell back on their alternate plan, leaving the bridge open at specified times. His alarm grew. For the next three days Hank couldn't sleep, spending most of his time at the control station. He lived on coffee and Tylenol. His nerves kept him wired up until his mind finally went numb.

The only things that came through the bridge were some stray birds, leaves, a rabbit and insects, all of which Hank managed to eject by sending them back. He began to panic. Is John dead? Where is he at? Maybe I can catch him just after he departed and bring him back before it's too late? He reset the machine to its original settings, and sent back the camcorder probe.

Hank felt the whirring sound and shudder from the machine. The probe was gone. He quickly brought it back and examined the film. There was smoke in the air. Hank could see smudge pots in the background. Lander had gone into the wrong time. If he is still alive, he is lost.

He felt a sense of helplessness and began experimenting with minute changes in frequency on the control panel. After each try he checked inside the chamber without result. The fluctuations in his settings became more wide spaced, until they were almost erratic. The last time he opened the door, it was filled with fog. The realization came to him. The bridge floats in its own continuum. No one can control time! He left the door open this time, walking back to the control station.

He was becoming confused, his mind growing numb from fatigue. "What do I do now?" he asked himself out loud.

A subdued sound came from the chamber, a guttural animal sound. Realizing he had left the door open, Hank advanced toward the machine. I'll close the door and send it back. Before he could cover the distance, the figure of a large cat appeared walking through the opening. It was taller than one would expect for its length, and its legs were short. It growled as it looked around finally fixating its eyes on Hank.

In disbelief Hank stared back. It had canine fangs projecting about seven to nine inches out of its upper jaw. Horrified, he stared at the beast. "Saber-toothed tiger!" he yelled. Backing up to the control station, he slammed the generators on full reverse power. Hank desperately hoped the beast could be sucked back into the chamber. The elevated sound only panicked the animal. It started running around the laboratory. Hank ran around the corner of the control station to a bolted door on the side of the workshop. This door could only be opened from the inside. He drew back the triple bolts as quick as he could. Then he opened the door wide, putting himself behind it as he did. The panic stricken animal ran past him and out into the night. Hank slammed the door and rammed the triple slide bolts closed. He powered down the machine. Still shaking with fear, he walked out of the workshop, and closed the door to the chamber.

Hank walked back to his house forgetting the big cat was also outside. Inside his kitchen, he sat at the table, contemplating this new situation. What have we done? What has John done? He must be dead. I killed him! And I released this primitive creature into our time. How much more damage have we done. What have I done?" Depressed, Hank thought of his PPK. "No, I don't want to go out that way. I just want out. Lander is dead and I'm all alone in this. I'll make my own way; I'm going into the future. I'm going home!

Hank returned to the lab and adjusted the settings at the control station. The frequency he chose was toward an opposite vector of time and space, away from the one Lander had gone to. This had never worked before. Never had they encountered a hit in that direction. He turned the machine on full, and locked himself into the chamber. With the whirr and vibration that followed, he was gone.

———

After that heart breaking goodbye with Charmaine, I had other, more pressing concerns. I had less than fifty dollars in currency on me, and only the clothes on my back. I took out my money, quickly checking the dates on the bills. None with a 1945 date! But this wouldn't take me very far either. I realized the irony of my situation as I picked up my grips and walked away from the phone booth. I paid premium prices for all of these coins. Now, I may have to spend them at face value to survive. At this moment, these other collectibles are almost worthless to me. One thing for sure, I had to get out of town.

I walked over to the red car stop. One came along shortly. I handed the conductor a nickel as I boarded and got off a few minutes later in downtown Los Angeles. I found a storage company on Alameda. Arriving twenty minutes before closing time, I managed to secure a storage closet, prepaying a year in advance. I divided my things into two groups. My most valuable collectibles would be in one group and remain here. I put some ready money, mostly in the form of silver dollars and smaller change in the other grip, also keeping some of the silver dollars in my pockets. I decided to keep my recall beacon with me. If I couldn't get back to pay the storage in time, I couldn't risk losing it; they might sell my goods. Although it had failed to work, the beacon was my only link to home. I felt some measure of comfort having it with me. I took a newspaper and stuffed it into the top of the grip I left in storage, placing Charmaine's sister's address beneath it. I double checked everything before I left.

Later that evening, I got off the red car in San Pedro. I made my way to that bar. There I met Mack, Leo and Milo. For me, that night was the beginning of World War II. Do I blame that chance meeting for my misfortune at sea? I don't think so. A thousand other bad things could have happened if I had chosen another direction. These guys became my true friends. I remember; they were so much fun.

chapter

8

AT SEA

I anxiously paced the foredeck on the cruiser waiting for these last four hours of sailing time to pass. Would Mack and Leo be alive, waiting in Darwin? How could my world of 2007 become a life at sea in 1945? Where would I be today if I hadn't met them? Remember, Lander? Remember how you became a seaman?

———

Macy Lamar Porter was thirty-three, sun bronzed and over two hundred pounds of trouble when aroused. Everyone just called him Mack. I got to know him about as well as anyone ever had during those next months. With his temper and willingness to socialize with ordinary seamen, he would never gain more rank. Mack had a hard time growing up and didn't talk much about

150

his childhood. We had an understanding about these things. I didn't ask him about his past; and he did the same for me. Still, bits and pieces of his life came out from time to time. When he was in his late teens and early twenties he had hardened his body working in a coal mine in western Pennsylvania. He had been at sea now for most of his adult life. Somewhere he had a wife and a son. But she had left him. He hadn't seen either of them in many years. Mack never learned how to treat a woman. To him, they were just broads. I reckoned if he had grown up in the '50s or '60s in Oakland, he would have become a Hell's Angel. He didn't have any smooth edges. He was rough and it didn't take anyone long to learn it. Mack didn't back down, or back up very far; no, not from anyone. But, one way or another, he was always there when I needed him.

Leo McGinty, on the other hand, was one of those characters one doesn't easily forget. He had to leave Ireland after the Easter Rising back in 1916. The British didn't like him very much. And when he described them he seldom used words longer than four letters doing it. Leo made his way to New York. Soon afterward he found his life's work at sea. He never had a wife. For him, every day was a new beginning. Planning for tomorrow never entered his head. The longest word in his vocabulary was whiskey. He could have fifty dollars in his pocket one minute and be as broke and naked as a plucked jaybird less than an hour later. But Leo was light and easy. He was fun to be around.

———

The first few days out, I was seasick all too often. Besides being sick, I didn't know anything. I was a deckhand or able seaman. As Bosun, Mack was able to protect me from unwanted questions. Then I started to pull myself together. I learned my duties quickly. As for the motion sickness, that passed too. I toughened. This was my first experience on the ocean. Movements that other seaman scarcely noticed made a big impression on me at first. The wind often raged, and the hull of the Roderick shuddered and creaked as the whole bow of our ship disappeared under the waves. It felt like the steamer could move in several directions at once. Frequently, the whole ship went into a trough, and then all other ships disappeared temporarily from our sight. The ship bounced, rolled, rocked, pitched and seemingly did all of these motions at the same time. The sound of metal slamming against the sea would make me wonder if she was breaking apart. And the screw propeller would sometimes come out of the water which increased its speed. Then it would slam back into the ocean with a shudder, and give us another unwanted thrill.

I lost my troubles in the rough and ready life of a merchant seaman, chipping old paint, and applying new coats where needed. I wire brushed the brass, repaired and spliced cables. I took my turn at the helm and stood my share of watches. I eagerly accepted these things, and all else that went with this job. We actually had it pretty good. A merchant seaman made a hundred bucks per month, compared to about fifty for an army private. And this pay doubled in war zones. Plus, we could make overtime. Making two hundred and seventy a month wasn't hard to do. I got regular food, a warm, dry place to sleep and a chance for fun and profit at every port of entry. We had an immeasurable amount of personal freedom compared to the armed services, no saluting, few titles, and lax discipline. All of these factors caused some jealousy from the Navy boys. They thought we were overpaid. It was remarkable though; a Navy Ship carrying the same cargo would have a crew of over three hundred. With only thirty-six men, maybe we were underpaid!

Milo was also a crewmember on the Roderick. But I didn't spend much time around him. The black gang worked in the engine room. We didn't share the same quarters. And I didn't see him very often. I was grateful for that. I was quartered in a room with the other three seamen on my watch.

Once I passed Milo as I walked down a rear ladder from the boat deck to the main deck. "Milo, do you still hold a grudge against me?" I asked.

He just looked at me and walked away. I never had trouble with him after that. But he never again bet against me in a crap game, either. Milo was quiet and moody. He never said much to anyone. Everyone knew he was dangerous. It was rumored that he had killed a man with a knife in New Orleans a long time ago, and spent some time in prison.

There were plenty of opportunities to get a game going. Most of the seamen on the Roderick liked to gamble. Mack, Leo and I almost always came out ahead. I even lost a little once in a while to make it look good. Even Milo turned it to his advantage when I held the dice. It wasn't just our own shipmates; the Navy boys liked to roll the bones too. I acquired a reputation. Soon, it became hard to get a game going. Poker was another favorite among the men. I stayed away from it. I was a put up or shut up guy. I had never learned the art of bluffing, or of reading people's expressions.

It was a long voyage to India. After twelve days at sea, part of our convoy split off and detoured for Apra Harbor in Guam. By the time we reached Calcutta, I had dropped fifteen pounds.

Johnny Grady's clothes no longer fit snug around my waist. The sea was good for me. The work could be hard but it kept my mind off my situation.

———

In Calcutta, our cargo of bombs was off loaded. Two days after arriving in Calcutta, the Roderick was nearly empty. Mack and I stood on the bow, watching the activity in the port. It was 16:00, our work day was over. Mack lit a Lucky Strike and looked over the scene as if he owned it. He always had that air of confidence, of being in control. "Know what Johnny?"

"What's that, Mack?"

"I was wonderin' if you would teach me that little trick with them dice."

"You finally got around to asking me. I knew you would someday. It's not as hard as it looks, Mack. If your point is a five, nine, six or eight, shake the dice around while they're still flat on the table, until you get a five on one die and a six on the other. Keep both on their horizontal axis, and align both dice together. Learn to look straight ahead, and watch them with your side vision as you set them. Try to conceal the movement with the top of your hand. And remember, Mack; don't shake them. Flick your wrist so that they come out spinning like a top. That spinning horizontal axis must be parallel to the surface they're going to land on. If they hit a flat surface they usually bounce off it directly, and fall backwards. It's better yet, if they land on a blanket or soft surface. This is called the blanket roll. Do it just right, and it will exclude the possibility of those surfaces on the vertical sides coming up. Even if you can't do it perfectly every time, this alters the odds in your favor. When you learn this move, Mack, you can make a six or an eight come up three times to that of a seven coming up twice. This also makes the five and nine an equal bet to the seven. If your point is a four or ten, align the one and the four axes. This makes a ten or four an equal bet to a seven." Mack grinned at me as he slowly exhaled the cigarette smoke. "But, remember this, Mack; don't try it in a casino. They are catching on to this technique. In a few more years, this move will only be a memory in casinos. They know it was used extensively in World War II." It was too late; I had done it again, spoken about the present as the past.

He looked at me. "You know, Johnny; why is it you sometimes talk about things like you was already there? Sometimes I just don't figure you out."

"Oh, it's nothing. I try to project my thoughts ahead and look back on things. It's just how I express myself."

"You still can handle them dice, Johnny?" Mack asked as he exhaled some smoke.

"I think so!"

"Wanna try the boys ashore?"

I nodded! "Know your way around here, Mack?"

"A good seaman always finds his way around, Johnny. If a guy can't find what he wants in a town this big, he ain't gonna find it nowhere."

"Who's our target, the Navy boys?"

"Army, Navy, other seamen like us, who cares? Everybody except the Brits, they never have any goddamn money anyway!"

"Let's do it, Mack!"

"Good, let's take a few bucks and pool our money; sorta like a business venture, you see. Then we'll go ashore and get acquainted. Here's what we'll do. I'll get a game goin' and lose a little money. I won't try to roll like you told me just now. You show up and I ask you to join in the play. You be reluctant see, but finally give in. When you get the dice, you bet small and don't take no odds. I'll increase the amount of my bets and then you turn on the charm with them dice. What about them apples, Johnny?"

I shook my head and laughed. "But no one suspects you because you're not holding the dice," I replied.

"You got it, buddy!"

"OK, Mack; let's get them!"

"Johnny, it'll be like we was fishing! I'll give them a little line and hook 'em. Then, you reel 'em in."

I laughed again. "Do we leave them with any skin on their backs?"

"Not much, Johnny. Big fish eat the little fish." He flicked his cigarette butt into the water and reached again for his pack of Luckys. "We're the big fish."

It was early evening. We three went ashore in our civvies. We only had four hours ashore. The Roderick was scheduled to vacate the wharf without taking on cargo. We walked into the teaming city. It looked like a pretty scary place to be all alone. The streets were packed with people going about on foot. And there were automobiles, bicycles and animals pulling carts every-where, even cows. The back alleys were even more crowded. I don't think I could get used to that smell in a whole lifetime. Filth, waste and stray animals could be seen everywhere. Never had I seen such a diversity of human types, turbaned men with beards, beggars, priests, coolies, prostitutes and orphans begging in the streets. There were immaculately dressed businessmen and British and Indian soldiers galore.

It didn't take long for us find a gin joint along the water-front. We could have crawled that far if we were desperate enough. We walked into Boomers and split up immediately. I went to the bar. Mack and Leo walked over and took chairs at a table next to a group of U.S. Army NCOs. By their patches, I could see they were in the Army Air Corps. Their table was littered with beer bottles. It was plain to see they were getting rowdy. The bar was filled with a variety of European types, some obviously down on their luck, the dregs of whatever country they hailed from. There were merchant seamen from a multi-tude of nations, and a variety of military types. Very few Indi-ans, other than hookers and waiters, were there. A couple of the women looked like Eurasians. I know one of them was speak-ing Russian in the corner of the bar. The large room was hazy with smoke and the sickly aroma of incense came through the back doors. Occasionally, a sailor would go upstairs with one of the girls. Others came back down. An Indian was playing a jazz tune on an old piano in the corner. If walls could talk, this place would have some great stories!

Without staring directly at Mack's table, I could see he had struck up a lively conversation with the GIs. It was pretty clear he fit right in with them. I was on my second beer when the whole lot of them, including Mack and Leo, got up and went upstairs. I nursed my beer along and waited.

Twenty minutes later Leo came back down the stairs and over to me, "It's time, Johnny!" He led me to a room upstairs. There were couches spread about. Girls of different colors were sitting about talking to the GIs. A corner of this room was crowded with NCOs in their dress khaki uniforms. I could hardly wait to see what they were doing.

I arrived in time to see Mack lose a bet. They were playing on a blanket. There was padding underneath it. I watched
the play. The Army boys were working together and using the
double-cross of the blanket roll on Mack. One of the sergeants
had the dice. The shooter's point was five. As he picked them
up, he placed a three next to a four on the horizontal axis before
making the roll. This would exclude the possibility of that five or
a nine coming up. Then, it was just a matter of time, until he sevened out. The conspirators could divide up Mack's money later,
and return theirs to boot.

"Gents, me friend asked if he could watch the game. It's new
to him. Is it alright with you boys?"

Without giving me a side glance, a couple of them said sure.
"Come on and have some fun, we'll teach you how to play."

"Oh, I'd just like to watch."

The Army boys were doing all right. Mack looked at me,
"Hey buddy, time to get your feet wet. This game is for men,
you're not at a picture show and you're not watching some goddamn baseball game neither."

"I'd like to try it at least once," I said.

One of the sergeants shoved the dice to me. "Sure!"

I pulled out my stash and picked up the dice. I made a two
dollar pass line bet, and threw them. I rolled a six.

Mack had put down a hundred. "I'm going to bet on his
beginner's luck."

"Odds?" asked the sergeant who was banking the game.

"What are odds? No." I replied. He allowed for single
odds only. Mack backed his bet with a hundred more. I couldn't
use the blanket roll on these guys. They already knew it. But
I could try the drop shot. These shysters weren't playing on a

hard surface. We had that much in our favor. I wasn't very good at this shot. But, I would have to make it work. Maybe I could tilt the odds, just a little.

"Hey buddy. I'll bet you even money you can't make snake eyes in twelve rolls," said another sergeant.

I smiled inwardly. "What are snake eyes?"

"The two, buddy. How about it?"

"Well, OK; here's a dollar."

The sergeant leered at me. "He's a brave one; ain't he?"

Mack butted in. "Can I take some of that action? Here's a hundred of mine."

"Sure, a man after my own heart, you're covered too pal."

I made sure the one was on the top side of each die. Then I stacked one on the other, and let go with the drop shot. No one recognized what I had done. On the third roll, snake eyes came up. Mack was elated. The Army boys were stunned.

Four rolls later the dice passed for me. The sergeant eyed me warily and paid us off. The dice passed for me four more times before I lost them. The game moved along. I managed to win three rolls for every loss. Mack bet small when I wasn't holding the dice. And, we cleaned up on some more proposition bets. Mack regained his losses, and was up five hundred. I was up forty!

The sergeant banking the game kept watching my play. "What's your ship sailor?" he finally asked me.

"The Roderick," I replied. Mack looked uneasy.

He turned to Mack. "Isn't that your ship, buddy?" Mack slowly nodded. You boys came into the canteen at the same time. This man goes to the bar and you other two came over by us. Next thing, you get a crap game goin' and this man shows up. Then you start winning big when he holds the dice. The sergeant stared into Mack's eyes. "Leave your money where it sits and get out!"

"I don't think so!" Mack replied, as he stood up. So did the sergeant. They were almost nose to nose. Mack's body as tense as an iron rod and the veins in his neck were protruding. He looked at me. "Hey, Johnny, think I should be afraid of this bird?"

I knew we had to have brass balls if we were going to walk out of there. The odds against us were too great. "Mack, it's pretty hard to be afraid of someone as butt ugly as he is!"

Mack laughed!

The GI scowled at me for a second, and then turned his attention back to Mack. "I said you're gonna leave the money and get out."

"Yeah, and you piss like a woman too."

The fight was on. The sergeant hit Mack between the eyes with the force of a jackhammer. He went down. I never thought Mack could get up; any ordinary man couldn't have. But I was wrong. Mack almost bounced off the floor as he came up and gave the GI a one two punch and sent him sprawling. Those years spent hardening his muscles in the coal mines didn't let him down now. I was hit also. But saw it coming, and it only glanced off my forehead as I stunned my opponent with a left hook. In what must have been a fraction of a second, Mack laid out another GI on his left. Cooler heads started to prevail. Some other sergeants grabbed their own and held them back. I looked around. Leo was lying on the floor, knocked cold. The whole exchange had lasted less than a minute. We had that to be grateful for. These boys were tough.

A sergeant with a Brooklyn accent spoke up. "We ain't even supposed to be in here. It's off limits. If we get caught gamblin' and fightin' we'll all get busted and go to brig. Let it go boys; it ain't worth it." Then he faced us. "Youse guys get out while you can," he said.

Mack answered him. "My money goes with me."

"Yeah, yeah, take it and get out." The sergeant who threw the first punch tried to argue with him, and had to be restrained. The Brooklyn born sergeant put his hands forcefully on his comrade's shoulders. "Let it go, Rooster; it ain't worth it."

A tiny trickle of blood oozed out of a cut above Mack's nose as he stared down the GI. The sergeant's eye was puffing up, and almost closed by now, but he still glared back.

"Mack, let's get Leo and get out of here." We gathered up our money, slung Leo between us and hastily sought new surroundings.

The Roderick left Calcutta empty. By the second week of February we were in the western Indian Ocean. This was unusual. We should have gone back to San Pedro. That's where this tour would have ended. Back in San Pedro, the seamen would turn in their cards at the union hall. When the call came for various specialties, the man who had been in port longest got the job. He could turn down up to two ships, then was obligated to take the third. Many seamen in the National Maritime Union didn't like working on the west coast. Most of these reroutings took place in the Pacific, and seaman could be gone for up to a year on this side.

chapter

9

CAPETOWN

he shoreline of Northern Australia was visible. We would be in Darwin within three hours. I prayed Mack and Leo would be there waiting. Leo! God, how did we ever win this war with him on our side? Oh hell, who cares; I love the guy, in spite of what happened in Capetown. Capetown I mused; I remember Capetown.

Entering the Office of the Commissioner of Police, Capetown, Union of South Africa, the British officer introduced himself as Major Palmer.

The police officer rose, and they shook hands. In flawless but highly Dutch accented English the policeman greeted him.

"Please have a seat, Major Palmer. I am Detective Leftenant Voorhis of the Criminal Investigation Division. I was assigned to work with you. I've carefully reviewed the intelligence briefs you sent me earlier today. Just this morning we picked up their operative in the shipping office. It didn't take long to break him. But he doesn't know the name or location of his contact. This agent communicates with him by making drops at specific locations. The Gray Shirts employ a child to make the pickup. This child then melts into a large group of children, and secretly passes it to another child and they scatter. After the Nazi agent receives the information, he passes it through the Spanish Consulate here. The information is encrypted and sent by diplomatic wire. The Nazis then radio back to their submarines operating in this theatre. It is round about, but they have had successes."

"Leftenant Voorhis, do you believe he might turn and work for us as a double agent?"

"To save his skin, yes! We worked a deal with him already. We instructed him to send one last incomplete message. Then, we made sure the word got out about his arrest. We hope this false information is tantalizing enough to bring this Nazi out of his hole."

"How do you propose to do this, Leftenant?"

"Major, I believe we can forge a path through Nazi sympathizers. We have plenty of them in South Africa. Unfortunately, a great many of my countrymen aren't very happy with our side in this war."

"Yes, I'm aware of that, Leftenant. So, how do we proceed?"

"There is a local man, Major Palmer, whom we believe has access to this German agent."

"So why don't you just pick him up?"

"We have nothing on him that would stick. He's not an enemy agent himself, though we believe him to be a closet Nazi. And the minute we pulled him in, he would cease to have value. The man we want would no longer associate with him. And for that matter, this would alert him to avoid the Nazi spy."

"So who is this individual, Leftenant?"

Voorhis handed a folder to Major Palmer. "It's all in there, Major. Franz Joseph Ostermann was born in Southwest Africa back in 1899, when it was still a German Colony. His father, who was born in Austria, had been a farmer in Southwest Africa until his death there in the 1920s. In the Great War, the younger Ostermann served in the German Colonial Army when he was only sixteen. He is not terribly fond of the British. He does have some friends well placed in the South African Government though. And, as I already said, we believe him to be a Nazi. He has ties to the local Gray Shirts, the pro-Nazi movement among some of our Boer population. Ostermann was also an associate of Oswald Pirow, the former South African Minister of Defense until late 1939. Pirow set up the New Order, which was designed to control South Africa along Nazi lines. They lost the election; South Africa remains loyal. But, they do have a lot of support remaining among our people. This Ostermann is an opportunist, implicated in dozens of crimes. I think we can use him, Major. I shall explain the details of my plan."

———

There was a shortage of British shipping in the Western Indian Ocean. Several U.S. Merchant ships were detoured to that area. The Roderick was one of them. By the third week of

February we were docked in Capetown, South Africa. Our triple expansion steam engine needed some repairs. This delayed us taking on cargo. Mack let Leo and me go ashore early on Friday. It was mid-afternoon as we stepped on the gangplank. I stopped and turned around to Mack who was standing on the far side of the main deck. "Are you going to join us for a drink soon?"

He shook his head. "It's gonna be a while. I gotta be here while the welders put up some posts for holding pens on deck. Seems like we're gonna take on some donkeys and mules later this week. You guys have a good time, and don't get in any trouble. And you, Johnny, watch out for Leo. He never did have much goddamn sense anyway."

Leo laughed. Nothing ever dampened his good nature. He pointed to Mack. "Ha, ha, ha! When you get through sweating up there, ye'll have a lot o' catchin' up to do." Mack's brow was already glistening with sweat; it was steadily growing hotter. Capetown is in the Southern Hemisphere, and this was February; it was summer.

Leo and I strolled down the gangplank and turned toward the waterfront district. We walked by sweating Blacks laboring over cargo in the turbid atmosphere of World War II in South Africa. I looked to both sides, trying figure out where we might go. "Leo, have you ever been here before?"

"Sure, Johnny me boy. Twice in twenty years, I think now! But I remember a good little pub not far from here."

We strolled a few blocks down Long Street until we turned into a narrow lane. Then we walked past a light chocolate colored girl standing by a pillar under an overhang. As we did, she gave us an inviting look. It wasn't a mental leap to figure out her line of work. Leo pointed to her. "The girls here what works this area is mostly colored as they calls them. Colored, that means half white, half black. But there's houses of white ones too."

"You mean prostitutes, Leo?"

"Me mother! Now what d'ya think I mean, Johnny? Did ye just leave the farm?"

"Leo, you're a real live sailor in the truest sense of the word."

"Now, what d'ya mean by that, Johnny?"

"I don't mean anything by it. You just live up to the image I always had of sailors."

"Anythin' wrong with that?"

"Nothing at all, Leo. Is this the place?"

"That it is, Johnny."

I looked at the sign above the door leading into the bar. It had a picture of a lighthouse on it, and the words *Die Vuurtoren* underneath. We walked inside. "I'll buy you a drink, Leo, unless you want to buy me one first." We had to go down three steps into a dark smoke filled cavern of a saloon. This wouldn't ever be classed as a four star joint in any tour book, but it had a certain something, a personality. A lot of diverse characters over the years had shaped the atmosphere here. We walked toward a small table near the window.

"Now for that drink ye promised, Johnny!"

"OK, Leo. We won't wait for table service. You grab the table." I casually walked to the bar and ordered two pints of dark porter and added a shot of Irish whiskey for Leo.

Within minutes I was walking back to the table balancing these three drinks. A svelte blond was sitting there talking to Leo. I sat the drinks down and smiled. Leo hadn't wasted any time! "Making a new friend, Leo?"

"Yes, Johnny, and she's a hell of a sight better to look at than you are." Leo hastily grabbed for his pint of porter.

I sat down and leveled my gaze at her. "Leo, you may have something there." I took a long draught of cool porter as I held her eyes with mine. It was pretty apparent that she wasn't very interested in Leo. How far do I let this go? Not far, I thought.

"Johnny, meet me good friend Christa."

"Kristol," she replied with a guttural accent, as she thrust her hand toward me. Nothing shy about this gal.

"Dutch?" I asked.

"No!"

"Boer, then?"

"No, German!"

"You're in unfriendly territory aren't you?"

"Not exactly, you see. I don't like the Nazis and they didn't like me for sure."

"I would have gotten you a drink, Kristol, but this is short notice."

"Would ye like to sip on me whiskey, Kristol darlin'?" Leo chimed in. With that invitation, she took his shot of whiskey, and downed it without a grimace. This was rich. That look of disappointment in Leo's face was priceless. I contained my laughter over his sense of loss.

This show was going to get good. Kristol was well known there. As we all sat together over the next hour, she held her own with Leo and me, drink after drink. It wasn't quite clear to me whether she wanted to hustle drinks for the bar or something else for herself. She didn't make any pitch to sell her charms. Occasionally, a new seaman would walk in and hoot something at her, and she responded in kind. This gal must have gotten over being shy before she turned fourteen. And, she probably lost something else in the process. I would have asked her what she did for a living, but wasn't sure I wanted to know. I was not surprised when she put her hand on my leg, and let it linger there for a while as we joked. It reminded me of my college days on a jaunt to Tijuana with my buddies, when I was sitting by a Mexican girl in a similar setting, and she grabbed for something else.

Leo left the table to go and relieve himself. Kristol reached into her bosom and pulled out a small handkerchief. She took a stone from it and shoved it toward me. I picked it up. It was a beautifully cut blue diamond. I knew it was well over one carat in size. "What's this Kristol?"

"Is very pretty, *ja?*"

"What are you going to do with it?"

"An associate asked me to find a buyer for him, darling. You like to buy maybe?"

"Why me?"

"Your friend Leo said you have money to buy things."

I was growing angry. "What else did he say, Kristol?"

"Only that you came in on the Roderick, Poopsie."

"Leo," I muttered under my breath. Mack's right; he doesn't have any goddamn sense. He doesn't think first, he just talks. Then the opportunistic side of my nature started creeping back in my thoughts. Diamonds! It's almost impossible to get a crap game going anymore. I don't know beans about diamonds, but I have a couple thousand dollars. Why not listen to her offer. "What's the deal, Kristol?"

"My associate wants two hundred dollars for it, darling. No questions asked! Are you interested?"

I was! "I have that much on me, Kristol. I'll buy the diamond."

"Oh, but I can only show it. Besides, he has more, darling. And he has to sell it to you himself. Would you like to meet him?"

"What have I got to lose? Sure, baby. Where do I find him?"

"I'll make a call, darling. I come right back!" She got up as Leo sat down.

"Where's she goin'? You didn't make her mad did ye, Johnny?"

"Leo, did anyone ever tell you that loose lips sink ships?"

"Johnny, I didn't say anythin' wrong; I just said we were from the Roderick."

"And you also told her that I had money. I swear, Leo; if I get mugged, I'm taking it out of your hide."

"Now, Johnny, to be sure, there's two of us; ain't they?"

"That's reassuring, Leo!"

"And you know how ye always said there's money to be made in the buyin' of ordinary things in these times. Didnya Johnny? I was only tryin' to be a friend and help."

"I guess I said that, Leo. But I don't like dealing with shady characters in foreign ports."

Kristol came back and sat down, looking pleased with herself. "My associate would like to talk to you darling, alone," she said to me.

"When?"

"He is coming soon now."

We were all feeling pretty good and loosening up when a portly man with a mustache and goatee walked in. He came right up to our table and spoke to Kristol in German. Then he walked away and took a table across the bar.

"Boys, he is my business associate."

"Doesn't he speak English? I asked.

"He does when he wants to, darling. Will you excuse me please?" She got up and joined him at his table. I could see Kristol was talking to him steadily. He was interested in whatever she was saying. He looked back at me twice. Soon they both came back. Kristol sat down.

He took off his rather well-worn hat and introduced himself. "*Bitte*, I am Herr Ostermann. I am from Southwest Africa. My parents were from Austria. But I am now happily a British subject and I often have business to conduct here in South Africa."

"What is your business, Herr Ostermann?" I asked.

"I buy and I sell."

"What do you buy and sell?"

"What I want to sell, what you want to buy! I would like to speak with you alone. I'll be at my table there." Ostermann returned to his table.

"What's this character all about, Kristol?

"He was a smuggler before the war, Poopsie. Illegal ivory, you know, and anything else he could make money on."

Leo walked to the bar for another round of drinks leaving her and me alone. "How do you fit into his plans, Kristol?"

"I don't, Poopsie; I just introduce him to interesting people. Maybe he pays me sometimes."

"OK then, how do we fit into his plans?"

"Not we, Poopsie, just you. Ostermann is not interested in your friend also."

"Why me?"

"He knows you came in on the Roderick which interests

him. Why, I don't know. Herr Ostermann also wants to unload some diamonds; this much I know."

Leo returned with a new round of drinks. "Leo will keep me company; won't you, darling?" He grinned and nodded. He also carefully placed his shot of whiskey beyond her reach.

"I'll be right back, Leo. I want to see what this Ostermann character has to offer." I went over to him. He motioned for me to sit down.

"Kristol tells me you have something I might want to buy, Mr. Ostermann?"

He abruptly nodded. "I am Herr Ostermann. Please do not call me mister. Kristol tells me you want to buy this blue diamond."

I pulled out two hundred and laid it before him.

He shoved the diamond toward me. "I have more in another place. I can get them for you. When do you sail?"

"We don't talk about these things, Herr Ostermann; I don't know anyway." He grunted and just looked at me. "I don't have all of my money with me. Most of it is in the ship's safe."

"I make you a good deal on others too, Herr Grady."

"I am Mister Grady; please don't call me Herr." I didn't know anything about diamonds but I knew that two hundred for the blue stone was cheap. "Where can I meet you in about an hour or so, Herr Ostermann?"

"Right here. We go from here together to a safe place. I must watch for police."

"I don't doubt it," I countered. "And Miss Kristol goes with us?"

"*Nein*," he said impatiently."

"OK, Ostermann; I'll look at the rest. But I don't make any promises to buy anything else. Understand?"

"*Ya, ya,*" he replied impatiently.

I repeated that I'd be back in about an hour. The blue diamond cost me almost all of my ready cash. The only reason I carried that much on me was the chance that I might find a lucrative crap game. I told Leo I was going back to the ship and get my money. He was sitting there laughing and getting toasted with Kristol. He waved me off, and I left.

Before going back to the ship, I inquired where I might find a jewelry shop. I was directed to one on Adderley Street. They appraised it and tried to buy it. I was astounded. It was a flawless blue diamond of almost two carats in weight. Was Ostermann really dense enough to sell at that price? I hurried back to the Roderick and turned in my receipt to the captain. He withdrew all of my money from the ship's safe. I had almost twenty-five hundred. But I didn't dare leave the diamond there. I tied it in a corner of my handkerchief. Before leaving the Roderick, I told Mack where to find us. I left the ship and was walking back up Long Street when men quickly grabbed me from each side. They were in plain clothes, but introduced themselves as constables. I protested in vain as they insisted I go with them, and then they shoved me into a waiting police car.

I was hauled into the Capetown Police Station and hustled into a room in front of two rather impressive looking officers. One was dressed in a police officer's uniform and he introduced himself as Leftenant Voorhis. The other was a British Army Officer. He introduced himself as Major Palmer, and he spoke with an educated British accent. As I stood in front of them with a constable by each side, my personal effects were placed in front of this British Officer. He methodically went through them, occasionally pausing to look at me.

After an interval, Palmer spoke first. "Mr. Grady is it? Seaman John Grady?"

"Yes, sir!"

"You are an able seaman on the Roderick, currently anchored near the new construction site of Duncan Wharf?"

"Yes, sir!" I answered again. "But what does a British Army Officer have to do with me? I'm not under your authority; am I?"

He carefully fingered the diamond I had bought from Ostermann, looked at me squarely and then turned and nodded to the policeman. "How about that question, Detective Leftenant Voorhis?"

Voorhis immediately responded. "Mr. Grady, you don't have a license to trade in diamonds, and besides that, trafficking in stolen diamonds is a serious crime in this country."

My heart sank. Is this what it has come down to, a prison in South Africa? "How do you know it's not mine?" I asked.

"Because, Seaman Grady, we know where it came from. It's stolen. And the only thing hotter than it right now is you, yourself. We've been on to you since before you had it appraised," said Voorhis.

"I really didn't know any of this was illegal," I lied.

"Yes you did, Seaman. Grady," he said confidently. "But I'm going to be generous; you're going to get a break. If you cooperate with Major Palmer, that is!"

"Just tell me what you want," I added quickly. I'll cooperate any way I can."

Voorhis told me to sit down. "How did you come by this diamond, Seaman Grady?"

I told him the entire story. I left out nothing or no one. I told him about Kristol and Ostermann.

After I finished, Voorhis spoke again. "We know you talked with him. You were being observed. We've been watching this Ostermann for some time now. We knew he was dealing in stolen diamonds. We've put up with his activities for a while, so we could learn more about his network. He has an associate we want to question. We need Ostermann to lead us to him."

"Why don't you just pick Ostermann up?" I asked. "And isn't this a civil or criminal matter? How could a simple thief interest the British Army?"

"He's not a simple thief, Seaman Grady," Palmer responded coldly.

"How do I fit into this, Major Palmer?"

"We're going to set up an operation against his associate, and you're going to help us."

"Why me?" I asked.

"You will arouse less suspicion than one of our locals," replied Voorhis. "Ostermann is a rather unscrupulous character. But we have to be careful how we handle him. We don't have solid evidence, as of yet. He does have some friends in the government, and we want to know more about his operation before we nab him. Besides trafficking in stolen diamonds, Ostermann has an associate that is extremely interested in the cargo of the Roderick. We have been feeding him tidbits to strengthen his curiosity. And, as he considers you to be just a nondescript American Seaman, you won't arouse his suspicion."

"What about it, Seaman Grady?" Palmer said sternly. "Or would you like the alternative instead?"

"I already agreed to cooperate, Major. Nothing has caused me to change my mind."

"That's the spirit," Palmer replied.

"Ostermann lives by no recognizable code when he makes deals outside of his circle of colleagues and friends," Voorhis added. "You are a mere mark to him, a source of quick gain."

"And he hates and despises you Americans almost as much as he does us British," said Palmer.

Leftenant Voorhis continued his explanation. I was to follow through with the diamond deal, and I would offer to sell valuable information about the Roderick.

"Isn't this a dangerous game, gentlemen?" I asked.

"Yes, they are going to kill you when they get what they want," Palmer answered.

My shock must have been electric; both Palmer and the policeman burst out laughing.

"We mustn't let that happen, Seaman Grady," said Voorhis. "We'll get you out. I hope. You see, when you discover the identity of Ostermann's associate, they don't dare let you return."

"What's my motive in volunteering to sell this information, sir?"

"Money! Ostermann already knows you're greedy."

"Your papers show that you were born in Ireland," Palmer added. "Throw in that tidbit and say they killed your father. Add that you hate the British. You never know, he might believe it! But strike the deal with him before you volunteer anything. You have to have something to sell."

I was to tell Ostermann's colleague that the animals being loaded onto the Roderick were only a cover story, to conceal the nature of its true cargo. The Roderick was going to be detoured to nearby Port Elizabeth, where uranium ore was going to be loaded into its holds, and shipped on to America. This ore was from Southwest Africa, and would be secretly transported by rail at night. Then, it was to be shipped via the Indian Ocean, where it would not be exposed to German Submarines. When I asked how I was supposed to have learned this, Palmer told me to say the Roderick's first mate was a drunk, who talked too much. Then Palmer asked me if I knew what uranium was. I lied and said no, which pleased him. Palmer added that he didn't really know what it was for either. I could see he was telling the truth.

"Am I supposed to know when the ship sails, Major Palmer?"

"No, that is too much; it's not believable. This colleague of Ostermann already knows anyway. He had a source in the shipping office. He had a source until a few days ago I should say."

"And if I go through the deal with the diamonds, will I get my money back?"

"We don't want your money, Seaman Grady. But you won't get to keep the blue diamond you bought," said Leftenant Voorhis.

"Can we talk more about my salvation? I'm not in a hurry to die."

"Ostermann will change cars at least once," said Voorhis. "This is a common tactic. We have a general idea of the direction he will take, and will have numerous unmarked chase cars waiting along the route we believe he will take. The hideout is in the Winelands, not far north and east of here. Before you make your rendezvous with him we need to fix you up with some special equipment."

"What is that, Leftenant? A pistol?"

"No, Seaman Grady. If there is any gunplay, we'll do it. We'll fix you up with a bright red shirt. You will hold your arm out of the window so that our people identify you and the car you're riding in. Our people will call ahead to the next lookout. In this manner, it will be a pursuit, but not a chase."

"And then?"

"Hopefully, Ostermann will lead us to this hideout, and we can spring you before they start playing really dirty."

"But I don't have a bright red shirt."

"I already told you we would provide one. It is lightweight, so as not to arouse suspicion," said Voorhis.

Palmer handed me my personal effects except for my dad's Masonic ring which he held in his hand. "Have you ever traveled?" he asked. I just looked at him dumbly. "You're not a Mason, are you, Mr. Grady?"

"It belonged to my dad."

"You know you really shouldn't be wearing this; don't you."

"Why? It's mine. Isn't it?"

"Well yes, I suppose if you look at it that way." Then Palmer frowned as examined it closer. "By the way, Seaman Grady, it contains the inscription 'Raised 7-15-70' inside the band. Was that your father's idea of a joke?"

I shrugged, confused at first. I didn't know what he was talking about until it hit me. I tried to contain my laughter as I realized the irony of it, 7-15-70. What an oversight! And I was going to be so meticulous about every detail. I told Palmer that my dad had been a Clamper and he enjoyed playing practical jokes.

"What is a Clamper, Seaman Grady?"

This is something I knew about. I was one. "It's a professional drinking society that almost went out of existence early this century, Major. But it is making a comeback. Our motto is Credo Quia Absurdum."

"I believe because it's ridiculous," said Palmer.

I stared at him in silent wonder. He speaks Latin too. Is there anything this bastard Palmer doesn't know?

Palmer looked at me skeptically, and handed back the ring. "Well, let's move on."

Palmer, the policeman and a constable led me to another room. They fitted me out a bright red shirt. "Remember, Seaman Grady, you must be sitting next to the window with your arm hanging out. After you change cars, you must make certain that you remain sitting next to the window. Our lookouts will see you and we can follow from out of sight. Pay attention to these instructions, Mr. Grady. You don't want us to lose you."

I was tempted to make a smart-aleck remark about wishing he had never found me, but thought better of it.

I returned to *Die Vuurtoren*. Mack was there. He motioned me over to him. A voluptuous blonde was sitting in his lap. "Hey, Johnny; come over here and meet my friend. This is Hennie. Say hi, Hennie."

She gave me an inviting look. "Hello, darling," in her accented English as she offered me her hand.

"Are you German too, Hennie?"

"No, darling, I'm Boer."

"Where's Leo?"

Mack pointed to our original table. "That's him over by the window with his head on the table.

I walked over to him. Leo was passed out cold. I looked back at Mack.

"Don't worry, Johnny. A couple of our guys are going back to the ship; they're gonna take him along." Looney and Moose walked over to the table. I helped them swing Leo between them. They left and I rejoined Mack. "Johnny, I'll bet Hennie here is willing to be nice to both of us." The blonde laughed and flung both of her arms around his neck.

"Sorry, Mack. I have business plans."

"Got a game?"

"No, you can't be part of this."

I couldn't see Ostermann anywhere. Then Kristol came walking into *Die Vuurtoren*. She saw me and came over to our table, and smiled at Hennie. Hallo *Hendrikje*."

Hennie replied, "Kristol darling!"

Kristol turned her attention back to me. "Ready, Mister Grady?"

"Tell Ostermann I am ready."

She somberly nodded and walked away. "I make the call now, Poopsie!" Five minutes later she returned. "Time now, darling; Herr Ostermann is waiting outside for you."

I followed her to the door and she pointed to him near a pillar. I walked up to him. "Mister Grady, we go for a walk now. I have the diamonds in a secret place. I must make certain we are not followed."

"Fine by me, Ostermann! I also have some information about the cargo of the Roderick that I'm willing to sell."

"What information is this?" he asked.

"I said for sale, Herr Ostermann. Johnny Grady is out for himself. I don't like the British any better than you do. I was born in Galway and they killed my dad."

Ostermann grunted with understanding. "How did you find this out?"

"The first mate is a drunk. He loosens up real easy when he's on the sauce."

"Mister Grady, you please go back inside and wait for me. I must make a call."

"Anything you say. But my information won't go cheap. I could be sticking my neck in a noose telling you this."

"We will see, Mister Grady."

I walked back inside and sat down across from Mack. Kristol looked puzzled. "You don't want to see Herr Ostermann's goods, darling?"

"There's more to it than that, Kristol. I'd rather not talk about it." I nursed a beer along. I was nervous but tried not to let it show.

A half hour later Ostermann walked back in and came up to me. "A car is waiting outside." We walked out together.

"You will bring me back here when we're done, right?"

"*Ya, ya,* get in please." A man stepped out of the back, and held the door of the old Citroen open. "Inside please," he said in heavily accented English.

"Please let me sit on the outside, I get car sick."

Ostermann was getting into the front seat next to the driver. "*Vas unsinn ist? A seaman gets sick from car ride? Amerikanischen Seemaner!*"

"I can't help it, Ostermann; I sit on the outside or I don't go." He nodded to his companions and the other man crawled in first. I found myself sitting next to two rather tough looking characters, and they weren't particularly friendly. "Where are we going?"

"You will see," one the men replied stoically."

Ostermann added, "You have the money?"

"Sure, but my information is more important than even your diamonds."

"We will see!"

There was silence for a while. We detoured into Adderley Street and followed it toward Table Mountain until turning on a side street. We changed cars here, and a decoy driver drove the Citroen off. Again, I had to insist on sitting by the window. I rolled it down and leaned my arm outside. We would soon be out of town. We drove north. The scenic backdrop of Table Mountain to our right was stunning. Capetown was a unique setting, strangely beautiful. A really beautiful place to die, I thought. How did I allow myself get in this mess?

About forty minutes later we were in the farm country. Ostermann looked over his left shoulder to me. "We are in the wine country; pretty, *ja*? We will soon be in *Paarl*."

I was really feeling insecure as I acknowledged him. At that moment I understood how a mob boss must feel, when he's taken for his last ride. Wild thoughts ran through my head. Maybe I should have let the Feds arrest me in California, and made a clean breast of it.

It was getting dark. We turned onto a series of dirt roads, and further on into a farm. From here on I knew we couldn't be observed by the police. It didn't matter anyway, as it had grown dark outside. The car stopped in front of a farmhouse, and we all got out except for the driver. We walked inside the farmhouse as he drove the car straight into a barn. Was this what Palmer wanted?

The house was old. There was no electricity, and only a lit kerosene lamp on the table. An impeccably dressed man with horn rimmed glasses sat at the table. Ostermann retrieved a bottle and glass, and sat down next to him. He motioned for me to take a chair opposite them. His goons took chairs by the walls on opposite sides from each other. Ostermann lit a cigar. His colleague somberly regarded me before speaking. "Seaman Grady, I hear you have some information of interest to me?"

"Who are you," I said.

"I am Herr Metzger. But who I am is of no importance to you. What do you have to sell to me?"

"Herr Metzger, the Roderick is taking on a strange cargo in Port Elizabeth in a few days and under unusual circumstances. But my information is worth something. I won't give it away."

He looked at me skeptically. "How much do you want?"

I had to buy as much time as I could. "How about a drink first, Herr Metzger?"

He nodded, and one of the goons brought a glass. Ostermann shoved the bottle toward me and I poured a stiff shot. Was this going to be my last drink? It burned its way down my throat.

"What's this?" I asked.

"Doornkat, Mister Grady, German gin," said Ostermann.

"First let me see what you have for sale, the diamonds you told me about."

"I think not, Mister Grady. You still have the diamond I sold to you?"

"No, it's on the ship."

He frowned. "You have the other money then, *ja?*"

Suddenly, I didn't want any part of this. "I do, why don't you just take it and let me go?"

"*Ya,* I will take it anyway, but we must talk also."

"What is the Roderick's cargo? asked Metzger. "It is better to cooperate. Then we will let you go."

It was time to play poker. "OK, Ostermann; I'll give you and Metzger here what you want. I'm sure we can make a deal."

"You will tell us all we want to know, and we make no deals," said Ostermann.

"We'll do it your way. You can have everything I know and rob me too, but at least give me one of those cigars, so I can calm my nerves."

He took one out of his pocket and shoved it toward me. I put it in my mouth and leaned toward the lantern. At that moment the driver came running through the door. He was yelling something in Afrikaans Dutch. He must have seen something he didn't like. If I did anything, it had to be now. I wouldn't get anymore chances. With a quick motion I grabbed the lantern, and threw it through the window. We were plunged into momentary darkness. The two henchmen grabbed me. I took some heavy blows to my head, but managed to break free after giving one of them an uppercut, and throwing the other one on top of him. I fought desperately, and for a moment got out of their grasp. I dove headlong through the window, and rolled through the fire created when the lantern hit the ground. One of the goons came through the door, gun in hand. I heard a shot. Was I hit? I didn't feel anything, but then I saw him fall. Men came running out of the shadows. Shots were returned from inside the house. The cops were here!

A man came up and helped me to my feet. It was Palmer. He shined a flashlight into my face. "You look like you've been put together out of spare parts, Seaman Grady."

My adrenaline was still pumping, and I barely felt any pain from the small burn I had on my shoulder. "Where the hell have you guys been? I almost got killed."

Palmer chuckled. "Everything worked out satisfactory, and you've kept your part of the bargain. You're lucky though, we lost your car a couple of times. Yes, I would say you're very lucky."

The gunshots tapered off. Ostermann and Metzger were apprehended running out through the back door. All of their henchmen were shot dead. "What about him?" I pointed to Ostermann as he was being led away

"I suspect he'll be hanged. I don't think he has anything more that we want. We have Metzger; that's who we were really after."

I glared at Palmer. "Is this what I think it is? You used me as a pawn to find some goddamn German agent? I want to go straight to my ship." I couldn't see the last of South Africa soon enough.

But first, I was taken back to police headquarters where Palmer and Voorhis debriefed me. Palmer went on to say that the American authorities would be informed of my cooperation.

This was something I couldn't risk. "Please, Major Palmer, I just want to live my life in peace. I'm no hero and I don't want any recognition."

He nodded to that. As he was finishing up the door to the office opened and Kristol walked in. Palmer and Voorhis seemed unperturbed. "Hello, Miss Meyer, please sit down and join us," said Voorhis.

My eyes got as big as silver dollars. Kristol calmly took a seat at a right angle to me. I rose to my feet and pointed to her. "She's the one who set up the deal between me and Ostermann. She had the blue diamond. She's the one I told you about. Arrest her!"

Voorhis spoke. "I think not, Seaman Grady. She is one of our most valuable operatives."

"But why didn't you use her instead of me?"

"She steered us to you. We needed an individual such as you, a seaman, to lead us to that German agent. The cargo of the Roderick was the bait, and he took it. Miss Meyer is far too valuable to risk in something as dangerous as this. She has the confidence of the local Gray Shirts. And, she set up the deal for Ostermann to steal those diamonds," he added.

I was stunned. "This was a put-up job," I said. With a dark look I stared into Kristol's eyes. "You played me, baby. I only wish I could do the same for you." She said nothing as she looked back at me with her laughing eyes.

"We'll have none of that, Seaman Grady. You have no idea what Miss Meyer went through in Germany."

I couldn't restrain myself as I lumped them together. "You Brits are a bunch of cold blooded bastards." Palmer smiled coldly. Voorhis was unreadable.

"Can I go to my ship now?"

"You can," Voorhis replied. "We'll make certain you get there."

"And you have the undying gratitude of His Majesty's Government," added Palmer.

I wanted to tell him what I thought of His Majesty's Government, but held back. Voorhis assigned another constable to escort me to the Roderick.

No bridge I had ever crossed in my life was ever as sweet as this one was, as I walked up the gangplank onto the Roderick. She was the only thing I could call home. Mack was waiting there at the top. He pressed me for information. "Don't ever ask me, Mack; please just don't ever ask me." I was going to go to my bunk, close my eyes and pretend none of this ever happened. I couldn't go on sticking out my neck like this. Gosh damn, I thought, does life have any more little adventures waiting for me?

We departed Capetown with a cargo of over 400 donkeys and mules bound for Calcutta. A contingent of soldiers to handle the animals also sailed with our ship's company. These handlers told us they were destined for a base called Imphal in Burma for service with the Indian Army. Before sailing into the Indian Ocean we stopped at Port Elizabeth and took on a cargo of corn, not uranium. Our five holds were filled with 7,000 tons of bagged corn the locals called mealies. It was a pungent trip. The donkeys were quartered in pens built on both the forward and aft decks. I told Leo that I was never going to another goddamn bar with him. I even kept my word until we reached the next port.

We sailed up the east coast of Africa to Aden. There we dropped our escort. The other merchantmen in our small convoy branched off and headed toward the Persian Gulf to re-supply the British Forces stationed there. This part of the Indian Ocean in 1945 was considered fairly safe; not every ship sailed in convoy from here.

It was in the evening on March 11th 1945, after a particularly hot and sultry day. We were about 600 miles east of Aden, occasionally changing course and zigzagging to confuse any unexpected submarine which we had been told wouldn't be there anyway.

I had just finished my watch on the bow at 16:00. The air in our quarters was thick and hot. I couldn't sleep in there and didn't even try. I grabbed a reed mat and my pillow and went topside wearing nothing but my pants. I was warned about this by my shipmates. Seamen even slept in their clothes and always had their life jacket within reach. I did not. I pitched the mat underneath the shade of the number three lifeboat on the port side. I would come out here often and sleep where it was cooler and I could catch a breeze. We all did. Seamen would sleep on top of the hatches and elsewhere on deck. Weather permitting, this was where most of our social time took place, card playing, chatting, spinning yarns, playing music and even the occasional game of chess. The Army and Navy boys joined us too.

As I lay there on my side facing the breeze, the wind caressed my face. It was still warm but it cooled me as I lay there thinking. I gazed up at the clouds. Lander, this isn't bad. I am making good money. We're due to return to San Pedro before May. I won't ship over. The recall from the machine is scheduled to begin in early June. I'll gather my goods from storage; use my earnings from the sea and place those bets I originally intended to make. It'll be a killing. I'll buy more collectibles and return to my own time. What about Charmaine? By now I knew it was too risky to try to live on both sides of the time bridge. I would return and stay in my own time. Charmaine? Would I have to give her up? No. I'll take her back with me. She only has her sister and grandparents here. Charmaine baby, I'm going to take what I want. I claim you for my own. I think she'll be happy with that arrangement. Anyway, this war was almost over. I didn't have much to worry about. I remembered reading somewhere that Japanese submarines preferred to target warships more so than merchantmen. And the Germans are in the Atlantic, so I'm pretty secure. Life is still holds promise; everything will turn out to be roses after all. I closed my eyes, visualized Charmaine and drifted off to sleep.

Later that evening, I awoke to the sound of torpedoes. And with them began my ordeal on the raft and brush with death in the Indian Ocean until I was rescued by this British Cruiser.

chapter

DARWIN

I leaned against the railing of the bow on the British cruiser enjoying the salt spray against my face. The cruiser was making its final approach to Darwin. I marveled how things could work out this way.

In Darwin I had to recap the story of the Jap sub to a board of inquiry with British, Australian and U.S. Navy Officers questioning me. They also informed me that the day might come when I would have to testify at a war crimes trial. I wasn't looking forward to that. Publicity is something that I didn't need. I knew that I would have to ditch this identity before that time ever came.

Out of ninety-two men on board the Roderick, only fifty-nine survived. In Darwin, I was reunited with Mack and Leo and the other survivors already there. They had been among those lucky enough to be picked up by the other British Cruiser. The British were hastily moving several warships through the Suez to Australia, and using Darwin as the staging point. It was apparent something big was going to happen.

Mack and Leo were thinner and sunburned from their ordeal, but in otherwise good condition. The three of us had a joyful reunion. Mack hugged me. "Well, Johnny, we're in the Torpedo Club now. We'll add a torpedo to our seaman's badge."

"It came at a big price, Mack. I wish someone else had the honor. But at least we can make our money the easy way until we get home."

Mack hesitated for a second as he looked at me. "Johnny, in case you don't know it, your pay stopped the minute the Roderick went down. The only thing extra you're gonna get is $300 to replace your kit back in Pedro."

"You mean the shipping company doesn't have any responsibility to us here?"

"Uh, uh, Johnny! We have to pay for our own food and lodging. All we're gonna get between here and San Pedro is a ride home, when there's one goin' that way."

I found this incredible. But those were the facts of life for merchant mariners in 1945. Transport on a U.S. Ship would be arranged for us back to San Pedro. The three of us had plenty of money between us. We would always have food and drink. And we helped some our shipmates who lost their money. That was the way of it, we were a brotherhood. We found cheap lodging, and waited. The authorities contacted the American Consulate and we were told we didn't have long to wait.

Sitting around, twiddling our thumbs wasn't our style. The three of us got really well acquainted with the local pubs. Word about my experience with the Japanese got around. Everyone wanted to hear the story about the Jap sub. I turned it to our advantage in these Aussie Pubs. There was always that element of con man in my soul. I traded stories for drinks, and they kept improving. I kept us in beer most of the time. The Aussies loved a good yarn. I wove the horrible reality of that event into a hero saga. The Aussies especially liked the part where we all gave the Japs an obscene gesture and cursed at them as we were being machine-gunned. Best of all, they loved the part where Jackson fired the flare gun at the Jap captain in his conning tower, burning him severely. I milked that story for all it was worth.

One morning I came across an American newspaper from the West Coast. I was incredulous as I read the story on page two. The FBI had detected more of those perfect counterfeit notes in Santa Monica. Their search had spread to the harbor area. A police artist had been able to draw a picture of me from witness statements. I looked at my likeness on the page before me. Suddenly, I wasn't looking forward to returning to the 'States. But there was no mention of my blonde companion being found either. Thank God for that. If I've brought ruin upon Charmaine, I swear I'll kill myself. I stopped reading and wondered what I should do? Once I arrive back in the 'States, it won't be long before I'm spotted and arrested. I'm in a fix. I walked the streets all morning trying to think of a solution. I couldn't go back yet. Should I hide here in Australia? No, I couldn't hide the fact that

I was an American. It wouldn't take long before the authorities started to ask me questions.

That afternoon I consulted with Mack. "I'm not ready to go back to San Pedro. Is there any way I can sign on another ship?"

"Could be," he said as he eyed me warily. "You weren't running away because you had two wives. Were you, Johnny?"

I just looked back at him.

"Hurt anybody?"

"No, Mack! I never hurt a man in my life. Or for that matter a woman or child. This is about money. But I'm not going to talk about it with you."

He lit up a Lucky. "Make off with the collection plate?"

"Ha, ha, ha! That's right, Mack!" We both laughed together.

"Merchant ships gotta have full crews. It's a union agreement. Want me check into it?"

"Could you do that for me?"

"Maybe I can handle it, Johnny. It ain't always easy." He said he'd be gone a while and left me alone. I forgot all about it until he returned later that afternoon. "Johnny, we're not goin' back to Pedro with the other guys. You and me and Leo are gonna ship out from here. There's gonna be a ship in port day after tomorrow that's short of men. The details is being worked out right now. This couldn't happen if there wasn't somethin' big gonna happen. They need men!"

"You got me through again, Mack. The debt sheet is piling up. I'm never going forget this."

"Oh shut up, Johnny; it ain't nothing no how!"

"Do they need a Bosun?"

"No, we're both gonna be able seamen."

"What does Leo think about it?" I asked.

"He doesn't know yet, Johnny, but we're keepin' him with us. Havin' Leo around is a little like smokin' cigarettes. He's a bad habit that you hate to give up."

"Suppose he doesn't want to?"

"Leo never knows what's good for him. We'll buy him a drink; that's the way to get to his heart."

"I think you're right, Mack."

It was the end of the first week in April. Our new ship, the Alma Rae, was to be unloaded before authorization came through for us to sign on. Later, we were told to report on board at 16:30 on the evening she was to sail. The ship's captain had to be certain that her three injured men could not sail on her. He wouldn't know this until the last minute. That was fine with us. We had a little more time to drink and carouse. We weren't told where we were going, just when to be on board. We visited Banty in the hospital for the last time. For him, the war was over.

It was our last morning in port before we reported to the ship. Leo and Mack went looking for the working girls like most other sailors did. I declined to go with them.

I could tell Leo was wondering about me. He looked worried and even asked me about it. "Don't ye like the girls, Johnny?"

"Sorry, guys; not this time. I'm homesick." No, I wasn't becoming a prude but I wanted Charmaine. Although I didn't think I would ever see her again, I didn't want to chance passing anything nasty on to her. But was she even thinking about me? Though I wished for it, I didn't have much real hope! But I made her a promise to return, and I'm going to play straight with you, Charmaine Baby. I could only wonder and wait, hoping she would do the same for me.

Leo put his hand on my shoulder. "Come on, Johnny. I'll even pay me self to get you one."

"Oh, Leo; enough of this! It's risky enough just going to a goddamn bar with you. Go have a good time. You can tell me about it later."

I parted company with them, slowly strolling with my hands in my pockets, leisurely looking over the wharf area. This is my last time in Darwin. I'll look it over once more. I headed down town and was soon walking on Daly Street. Darwin had taken some bomb damage early in the war, but most of it was intact. Resembling a frontier town from the last century, it bustled with military activity. The air was sticky and heavy; we were still in the tropics. But Darwin was nobody's idea of a tropical paradise.

I walked by a shop on Daly Street. Its sign read Chemist. We would call this a drug store back in the 'States. Though I seldom ate candy, I felt the impulse to buy something sweet. Their stock was limited and mostly consisted of non-prescription drugs. I leisurely walked inside and stopped by some old photos. Why not buy a souvenir? My memories of this town would be nice. I selected a few, and carried them to the counter. There was a pretty, dark haired girl working behind the cash register. She couldn't have been much more than eighteen. The proprietor was in a back room.

"Do you have any candy here, miss?"

"Sir, we have a small selection. And, some American chocolates too! Do you like Hershey bars?"

I looked at this pretty creature and asked her name.

"Meghan, sir! Meghan, with an aytch!"

"Meghan, with or without an H, you're a very pretty girl."

The girl shyly looked down, and then back up at me, smiling. "Thank you, sir." She was refreshing and reminded me of my own Charmaine. That's funny, I mused, my own Charmaine. She probably thinks I abandoned her long ago. I suddenly became depressed and angry inside with visions of her being touched by other men. I forgot about the candy and passed the next twenty minutes flirting with this pretty dark-haired girl. I could see her employer was getting restive and knew I had to break this off.

"I had better get going, Meghan. How much for these pictures?"

"They're sixpence each. Are you going to the tea this afternoon, sir?"

"What tea, Meghan?"

"The one at the Catholic Church, for the Americans at 2:30."

"Meghan, I've never been to a tea in my life! I didn't hear anything about it, and I wasn't invited. Besides, if it's for servicemen, we merchant seamen wouldn't be allowed there."

"All Americans are invited, sir. I quit at two today. I could walk you over there when I get off."

I looked at the clock on the wall. It was 1:35. I was in no big hurry to part company with this girl. She had a natural sweetness and innocence that I missed in Charmaine. "If I go, Meghan, enough of this sir stuff; call me John!"

"Yes, sir, John! I won't be a minute!"

I waited for her across the street, where I shared a bench with a grizzled, heavily bearded old timer. He had been born just after our own civil war. He was a genuine frontier type, not

like the wannabees I had known in my own time. If only I were
a writer, I could have turned his stories into gold. He kept me
entertained for the best part of a half hour. I excused myself
when Meghan came out of the shop.

"I brought some candy for you," she said. "Here, John, try
one. It's peppermint." I took a small piece. She was vivacious and
enjoyed talking. I listened to her innocent stories with pleasure.
The girl had just turned eighteen, and was becoming aware of
her womanhood. We approached the Catholic Church where
her family attended. "That's it there; we can go in now!"

"It's only ten after two, Meghan. I don't feel like sitting
down yet. Can we walk for a while?"

"Oh, that sounds like fun! John, where is home to you?"

"I don't reckon I can call anyplace home, unless maybe it's
the sea."

"Are you married, John?"

"No."

"Where do your people live?"

"I don't have anyone there I can call my people just now,
Meghan."

"You're a sundowner then," she replied.

"What is that, pretty baby?"

"Your home is where the sun sets."

"Ha, ha; I guess so, Meghan!" She was a gentle creature. We
walked on and lost track of time. There was no more mention of
going to tea. I enjoyed listening to her talk about her world.

"You're different from Australian men. They're not interested in a woman's opinion. It's so easy talking to you, John."

"How is that, Meghan?"

The Northern Territory is a man's world."

"Were you born here?"

"I was. Someday I'm going to leave though."

"Why, Meghan?"

"Darwin is the only big town I've ever seen. I know there's another world out there. I see it at the cinema."

Strange, I thought; she thinks Darwin is a big town. The afternoon passed by much too quick for my liking. I looked at my new watch; it was four. "I must report to my ship in a half hour, Meghan."

"I shan't look forward to that. This has been fun for me too."

She flashed me a smile that made me wish I was the boy next door. The old Lander wasn't dead. I felt the blood flow in my loins. Australia would be a fun type place for a guy like me. "You're a very pretty baby, Meghan; but I have to go now. I'll walk you home first."

"John, it wouldn't be good for me mum and me dad to see me walking with an American sailor."

"I'll say goodbye to you here then."

"No, please, can I walk you to your ship?"

"OK, pretty baby; a guy can't turn down an offer like that!"

We walked to the entrance of the Naval Base. An Aussie soldier with a bayonet on his Enfield, stood there on guard. "Going inside, myte?"

"Right away!" I answered. My friends were waiting for me inside. I turned and faced the girl. "This is goodbye, pretty baby. There is a big world waiting out there for you. It's beyond Darwin, but you'll find it." I took her hand, raised it to my lips, and kissed it. I could see she wanted more of a goodbye. I gently pulled her into me and kissed her on her lips. They were moist and responsive. I could feel her excitement. But her expression was one of wonder. This must have been her very first kiss. I left her there, and she watched me with her lips slightly parted as I walked past the guard. She waved one last time when I turned around after stopping by Mack and Leo. She stood looking at me for a minute, and then quickly walked away. Meghan had a lot of growing to do. I hoped she would find the right guy to do it with.

With their jaws hanging slack, my friends had been watching me say farewell. In the forthcoming weeks their questions grew tiresome. They never did quite believe that nothing had happened between us. If I were a younger version of Lander, who knows! Maybe they would have been right.

We walked down the quay until we reached the Alma Rae. Our amazement was mutually felt, as we stood there looking at our new ship.

Mack grimaced. "She ain't much to look at! I wonder how the food is."

"Leo shook his head. Where did they dig that up? It's nothin' but a goddamn Hog Islander."

I glanced at him, then turned to Mack. "What's a Hog Islander?"

"Just an old ship, Johnny, too small to be profitable for ocean traffic any more. They're mostly used along the coast, carryin' things like lumber. Who knows what else? Yeah, she's a real tramp, probably worked in the islands before the war, shallow draft. These tramp steamers can sometimes get up rivers where a big ship can't go."

Leo bellowed at the top of his lungs. "This goddamn scow probably hauled pineapples and coconuts. I ain't goin' with youse guys. I'm goin' back to 'Pedro. That's all there is to it."

Mack grabbed his right arm. "Yeah you are, Leo." I took his left arm. Then we lifted him off the ground between us, and carried him up the gangplank. We three signed the articles just minutes later. We were the newest able seamen on the Alma Rae. She was an older steamer of 3,000 tons, built more than a generation before the war.

The ship had been strafed by some Jap planes on her voyage near Bougainville. Three of her seamen were badly hurt in that attack. They would remain in a hospital in Darwin. Strangely enough, the ship wasn't taking on any cargo. Whatever we were supposed to be loaded with, it wasn't here in Darwin.

chapter

11

NORTHWARD INTO HELL

I would have to form a plan for my future. I was really stranded in this era, probably for good. There was little reason to go the recall point. I didn't have my beacon. It went down with the Roderick. Hank and I were out of sync. He wouldn't know when to open the bridge. If he has opened it to May or June already, he's probably surfing through time looking for my signal. I could sit for months in that same spot in the orange grove and still not make contact with him.

A plan began coming together. I'd go through the remainder of the war and add to my stash. I would have to become part of life in this here and now, more or less permanently. Technology would have to catch up if I had any chance at all of going home. But even the transistor wouldn't be invented until the '50s. Did I dare risk being creative and try to replicate certain technologies before their time? No, I wouldn't just be drawing attention to myself, but inviting examination of a past that didn't exist. I might also mess up the natural development of technology by interfering with its true inventor. I might not even live to the point in time where certain materials would exist to recreate the technology that brought me here. Even if I did, I had no idea how Hank's magnetic polarization box worked or was composed of. I certainly wouldn't make it if I continued having these unwanted adventures. Those collectibles I had gathered wouldn't begin paying for themselves for a long time. But I knew just enough about the '50s and '60s to pave a golden future. Honestly, away from this damned war, I loved it here. My immediate concerns were survival and anonymity Then I could dare think about reuniting with Charmaine? I put her out of my head for now, as much as I could.

Darwin was filled with British, Australian, Dutch, and American ships. There were combat naval vessels, all kinds of auxiliaries, and merchantmen like us. Our convoy was nearly assembled and ready. All of the ship's bunkers were finally topped off from the oil tunnels. Back in 1941, these tunnels had been built to protect the vital oil supply after the Japanese bombing attack. Darwin was a strategic port. We found out we were going to rendezvous with more shipping and pick up additional escort vessels somewhere else. We could only guess what future lay in wait for us.

That same night we finished making ready to sail. Mack and I were working on deck. It was an unusual thing, but I felt the need to talk, and about things that didn't normally get said. "I've got a goal, Mack. And someday soon, I hope to get it. When I do, the dice go on the shelf forever."

"Got a gal waitin' for you; don't you Johnny?"

"Yeah, you could say that. This war's going to be over some-day soon. I just hope that certain someone is still waiting for me."

"I know you don't like talkin' about your past, Johnny; but what's her name?"

"Charmaine!"

"This war's gonna go on a long time, Johnny. Them god-damn Japs'll never surrender. We're gonna have to invade Japan and kill every one of them bastard sons of bitches. You got plenty of time to get over her."

"Invade? No we're not. This war will only last a few more months."

"Are you projecting yourself again, Johnny?"

I laughed, looked over the rail and down into the water. "Yeah, I guess so."

Reaching for the inevitable Lucky Strike, he stopped what he was doing as he looked at me. "Johnny, the sea is the only wife a man really needs. She gives us a good livin' and a seaman can always find a warm body in some port."

"Some men need a little more than that in life, Mack. Your life at sea is really simple and I know some men crave that. There is another life waiting for me. I look forward to it. All I have to do is survive this war and get there."

By 21:00 on that last evening in Darwin, the first ships of our convoy were leaving port with escorts taking the lead. Days of sailing lay ahead of us. I leaned into my work these next several weeks with a vigor I had never felt before. I knew I was trying to hurry up the months. It didn't work that way, but it was good for me to stay busy.

We put into Leyte. Here, the serious work began. It would be many weeks before my feet again touched land. The loading facilities at Leyte were strained, but it was apparent we were given priority. The combat loading teams worked around the clock. These teams were composed exclusively of Black GIs. The polite term in those days was colored. Our four holds were filled full of construction materials within twenty-four hours. We must have been important, extra men were assigned to the task. On our rear deck, large cranes hoisted the biggest rock crusher I had ever seen. The foredecks were filled with earthmoving equipment. The little Alma Rae was not equipped with the same guns as the bigger Liberty ships were. Welders came on board and welded extra stanchions onto our deck in several places. These were machine gun mounts. In all, we were re-equipped with an additional four fifty caliber guns, which made a total of eight. By the end of the last week in April, the Alma Rae was again heading northward, well out to sea.

Some of the ugliest combat of the war was taking place by the first of April in 1945. I had never been particularly interested in history. I had heard of this battle of course. But all of this was still new to me. Americans were being killed and wounded by the tens of thousands in the biggest battle fought in the Pacific. Most of the Japanese would be killed. Their code of Bushido forbade them to surrender. Marines, GIs and Japanese alike were going through this meat grinder of hell on an island that was going to be known as the Battle of Okinawa.

———

It was in late April, 1945. The Marine guard snapped to attention and saluted. He had a holstered '45 at his waist. The lead officer returned his salute. The Marine reached over, opened the wardroom door and stepped aside. The officers entered the wardroom. Immediately, all officers inside snapped to attention upon command. "At ease," said the senior officer. Before walking to the head of the table, he took off his saucer hat heavily laden with gold trim and added it to the collection of hats already on a side table. The officer following him did the same.

As he reached his chair, Admiral Nimitz said, "Take your seats, gentlemen." All sat down except for his adjutant who began distributing documents among the dozen senior officers present. All branches of the armed forces were represented there. A colored steward came in with cups and coffee. Ashtrays were spread about the table and most of the officers were soon smoking. His task completed, the steward left the wardroom and it was secured from further intrusion.

"Gentlemen," began Admiral Nimitz, "We have effectuated our initial invasion movements in Operation Iceberg. I'm ready for your reports now." One by one the various officers covered their areas of expertise: intelligence from aerial photography and radio intercepts, weather, fueling, re-supply, troop transport, aviation, ground combat, maintenance and so on. Nimitz interrupted sometimes with questions, other times with observations of his own. Nimitz had been brilliant in battle. He was also lucky and he had a star studded team of subordinates working under him.

There was urgency in this meeting. "Gentlemen," continued Nimitz, "Our losses are mounting in this battle for Okinawa. This campaign is behind schedule. Soon we'll be invading the Japanese Home Islands. Okinawa is critical to our invasion plans. When that time comes, American blood will flow like water. When our boys hit those beaches on Honshu Island we have to support them with everything we've got. These air bases on

Okinawa must be finished to handle the B-29s. Overwhelming air superiority will be the key to our ultimate victory over Japan. Otherwise the invasion will be an even greater bloodbath for our boys. I am sure you all understand the urgency here. These Japanese, as you all know, are prepared to sacrifice millions of their own. And they plan to stop us on their beaches."

Nimitz turned his attention to Admiral Spruance. He was Commander of the 5th fleet, and had replaced Bull Halsey after the devastating hurricane in December of 1944. That hurricane had almost led to Halsey's court martial. Though old friends with Halsey, Nimitz couldn't help but remember the massive damage to the fleet as he looked at Spruance. Well, I was able to save Halsey, Nimitz thought. He looked at Spruance and wondered; he's come a long way since being a cruiser captain. He had no experience with carriers before the war. "Admiral Spruance, how are we progressing with those airfields?"

Ray Spruance felt the pressure of command. Operation Iceberg's initial success lay on his shoulders. He was the invasion commander in the early stages of the campaign for Okinawa. "Admiral Nimitz, We have been able to recondition the Kadena and Yontan airfields. But they are in very poor condition. The Japanese only surfaced them with a thin layer of coral and the drainage is totally inadequate. There are numerous sites suitable for the construction of bomber and fighter bases on Okinawa alone. We could more efficiently concentrate our efforts there and abandon some of our Phase III plans for bases on the surrounding Islands."

"Do you recommend that we abandon plans for all of those islands, Admiral Spruance?"

"No, sir! I recommend we keep Ie Shima for fighter bases."

"Then, progress is being made to recondition those existing bases on Okinawa, Admiral Spruance?"

"There are logistical problems, Admiral Nimitz. The coral currently being used for resurfacing is of very poor quality. As of yet, we don't have a rock crusher available to take advantage of the limestone quarry on Okinawa. There is also good quality rock there in the old Shuri Castle. We plan to make use of it too."

"Why hasn't a rock crusher been made available to our engineers?"

"I believe Admiral Turner can answer that better than I, sir." Spruance nodded to Turner, "Admiral Turner?"

Admiral Turner was in command of logistics. He was the genius of supply. "Landing difficulties, Admiral Nimitz, but this is being worked out as we speak. This single piece of equipment alone weighs one hundred tons. Preferably, we need the port facilities at Naha, but haven't taken that port yet. We anticipate it will be in our hands within days. We need a shallow draft vessel. The Japanese have sunk a lot of ships in Naha Harbor. And there are mines and other obstacles too."

"Where is this crusher coming from, Admiral Turner?"

"We're getting one from Leyte, sir."

"When will it become available, Admiral Turner?"

Turner nodded to a captain sitting across from him, "What about it, Captain Fuller?"

The captain promptly answered. "Admiral Nimitz, there's an old steamer, the Alma Rae that will be arriving in Leyte tomorrow. She has only 3,000 tons burden and doesn't draw much water. She will be loaded with the rock crusher and some other engineering equipment. The ship will arrive in convoy within

two weeks. By the end of the third week of May, this machinery
should be unloaded and already in use by our engineers. The
rock crusher is so heavy, that we need the wharf at Naha. We
considered unloading it at one of the sand bridges being con-
structed into the ocean. But if the weather turns bad and these
land bridges become saturated, the multiple wheeled transport
dolly will sink into it under the weight of that crusher.

The conference continued. "Gentlemen," concluded Admiral Nimitz. "I am going to make the necessary recommendations
to the Joint Chiefs of Staff to concentrate our airbase construction on Okinawa and Ie Shima. Do any of you gentlemen have
anything else at this time?" All officers present shook their heads.
"If no one among you has anything to add, this conference is
concluded." As Nimitz stood up all of the officers arose to attention. Nimitz, followed by his adjutant, retrieved their hats and
briskly left the ward room.

————

By the beginning of the second week in May we were near-
ing our destination. It was clear that our course was holding
steadily northward. I thought the war was winding down. But
the battle for Okinawa was in full swing and it was our fate to
become part of it.

We arrived off Okinawa. We didn't know it then, but there
had been delays. Our formation lingered for days, several miles
off the beaches. Throughout these days and into the nights,
we could hear the thundering of the battleships' big guns. We
could see the smoke they belched during the hours of light and
the flashes of crimson light spewing from their barrels at night.

Planes beyond counting filled the sky, and we saw hundreds of them falling as they trailed plumes of smoke. These kills were mostly Japanese Kamikazes, but our destroyers were taking an especially big hit from them. Several days passed by; all we could do was wait. The last part of May and early June were miserable with excessive rain. I knew those Marine and GI Grunts were going through hell.

We had plenty of time on our hands; all of us listened to Tokyo Rose. I had grown fond of the music of this era. Before coming to this far place in time, I never gave big band music a second thought. Here, it grew on me. The switch inside my brain had flipped. I was now a man of this generation. Tokyo Rose was always good for a laugh. We listened to her tell us how our forces were being repelled on Okinawa. She said all of our ships were being lost to the Divine Wind of the Kamikazes. She reminded us that the boys back home were getting our girlfriends and wives. Well, Rosy old girl, you're probably right about this last part!

These same exceptionally heavy rains delayed the unloading of our equipment. But when our turn came, things happened quickly. It was the end of the first week in June when the word finally came down to us. The Marines finally captured Naha, but well behind schedule. The Japanese destroyed its port facilities. They would have to be rebuilt. And the harbor had to be cleared of sunken Japanese ships before our large ships could put in there. The Navy boys wasted no time getting started. Soon enough, small ships could reach the wharves.

The time for us had come. By first light an ocean-going tug nudged the Alma Rae inshore close by the main wharf at Naha. A crane barge was anchored between our ship and the quay. The Seabees were hungry for this equipment and were working together with the combat loading teams. Special made dollies with multiple wheels had been prepared for the rock crusher.

It was still early, not quite 07:00. A cacophony of harsh sounds began as hundreds of guns began filling the sky with shellfire. Someone yelled, "Kamikazes!" I looked toward them. It was a flight of between seventy and a hundred planes of different shapes and sizes. They were going for the transports. They were also being shot out of the sky almost as fast. One of them dove toward the Alma Rae. The cry was heard, "Incoming!" Our small fifty calibers were pouring a rain a fire all around him. He kept coming as he trailed a plume of smoke. From my position near the bow I could see he was aiming for the bridge. The pilot poured a rain of gunfire into it. Immediately, Captain Robeson, the First Mate and everyone on it were killed.

Just moments before impact, the plane began to veer slightly to port, and almost missed us totally. I temporarily lost him when he passed out of my line of sight as I stood on the foredeck. Then came the wrenching sound of metal colliding with metal. The left wing from the Japanese plane was sheared off by our foremast. Just beyond our deck on the port side, the Jap plane exploded. Its shards of death spread over our foredeck killing and wounding more than two dozen men. The flaming wing fell to the deck. The men working immediately under it were killed. I was working on some turnbuckles near the number one hold when it exploded. The bomb's shrapnel missed me but the concussion from the explosion propelled me headfirst into a winch. I felt a warm trickle of blood going into my left eye. I didn't waste any time thinking about it.

The Alma Rae was on fire. The Bosun was dead. Our Second Mate, Van Hoeven, was not on the bridge when the Kamikaze strafed it. He quickly ran to the foredeck, took command and organized teams to fight the fire. I got up and ran back to one of the fire stations by the superstructure. All available seamen were scrambling for the fire hoses. I held one while another seaman worked its nozzle. The gasoline fire from the wing had spread to the number two hatch cover. We poured a stream of cold water over it. The hatch cover was almost destroyed, but we had to prevent the gasoline from burning through it into the number two hold. There was too much flammable material down inside.

Without waiting for orders, Mack released the final turn-buckles holding down a D7 crawler. He jumped onto it and fired it up. Within the short confines of space that he could maneuver, he drove it through the burning aviation gasoline. He caught the blade of the dozer against the wing and shoved the throttle full forward shoving the wing away from the deck machinery. Steadily the D7 pushed the wreckage until it went over the side. Mack's clothes were on fire and I knew he was hurt bad. He shut down the D7 and jumped to a clear section of the deck where he ripped off his pants. Burns covered the lower part of his legs.

Again, all of our guns and hundreds more from the surrounding fleet opened up. Another Kamikaze was diving toward our ship. A navy gunner at the nearby fifty caliber machine gun fell as gunfire from the Jap plane raked his position and cut him down. The sailor had just finished changing out the hundred round box of ammo and cocking his gun. I glimpsed another Navy boy running to the unmanned gun. He didn't make it, and was cut down too. All of this taking place within seconds, I ran toward the gun with a sense of desperate determination. I had no desire to be and would never classify myself as a hero by anybody's standards. I reacted instinctively as I grabbed for the dual handles on the fifty caliber's breech. With my thumbs, I pressed the firing levers and sent a stream of fire into the Japanese plane. It was now only a few hundred feet away. Shells were landing all around me. The Jap Pilot was guiding his plane to hit us low amidships. If he made it, the Alma Rae's hull would be blown up at the water line. She would go down. I emptied the gun's magazine as I watched the tracers crisscross in front of him. At the last possible moment, the Jap plane started trailing smoke as metal fell from its engine. It slightly altered course toward its right. Then it crashed into our upper bow, blowing a fifteen foot section away. But the Alma Rae remained afloat.

I figured if we could survive this day, we would have our ticket back to Pearl. We did, and it was. All of the deck machinery on the foredeck was damaged and unusable. I would always carry a three inch scar above my left eye from this battle. Call it fate; I don't know. I had just walked down another road in life. But I would live.

In late July of 1945, we were in Honolulu. The Alma Rae had been removed from temporary dry dock. She was scheduled to be sent on to San Pedro for final repairs. Mack would be released from the burn ward today. I planned to meet him at the hospital. I had faced a pang of conscience. Here I was. I had always been selfish to the core, always looking for an easy way to make money. I had to do at least one thing worthwhile in my life. I remembered the horror I felt when I was floating that night in the Indian Ocean, when I was one breath away from becoming some shark's dinner. Words had different meanings to me now.

These weren't just abstract scribbling on the page of some book. What happened to the old Lander? Never before had work, duty, honor, hunger, thirst, love, and friendship meant so much to me.

Then I knew what I must do. I took out pen and paper and crafted a letter in block printing, which I left unsigned. I addressed it to Commander-in-Chief Pacific Ocean Areas Forces in Honolulu. I finished it without any return address. I didn't mail it from the ship. That would be too risky. I dropped it off at the main post office in Honolulu. I knew it would be opened by someone lower in the chain of command. But I hoped the information would find its way to the top. I described how the USS Indianapolis would be carrying the first atomic bomb to be used against Hiroshima. And, that it would be torpedoed on its way to the Philippines, shortly after returning from delivering it. I described how most of the crew would be eaten by sharks, unless the Navy did something to prevent it. I knew it might change the course of events somewhat; but I had already done that many times myself. I wanted to give those men a chance to live, and not face that horrible end.

A couple of weeks later, I learned that the Indianapolis went down just as it had before, and under the same circumstances. I had not been able to save them. Did I have a hand in this? I didn't know. Fate moves in strange ways. I was haunted by the vision that I might have played a part in the disaster because of the letter. I resolved that I would never try to influence world events again. If I did, I might become part of the problem. Days later, to my relief, I learned that the disaster was caused by a bureaucratic screw-up. Those men remained in the water all those days, because the ship was not reported overdue. I would never know what became of my letter.

We had one last night ashore in Honolulu. Mack found a big crap game downtown. At first my heart wasn't in it. I relented. It was a good thing, too. I doubled my stash. Whatever future lay in store for me on the mainland, I wouldn't have to immediately sweat for lack of money.

This was now early August, and we were at sea heading for San Pedro. The prospect of seeing Charmaine was constantly on my mind. I felt low in spirit as I thought the situation over. She thinks you're long gone, Lander. What normal, vibrant girl would wait this long? She has probably taken up with a young man by now. And why not? I'm fifteen whole years older than her. She must believe that I stood her up. I tried to argue myself out of this line of thinking. One thing was for certain though; I had to know. I'll go to her sister's house and try to locate her.

chapter

12

IT ALL COMES TOGETHER

Our ship arrived in San Pedro. We soon docked and were paid off. The Alma Rae would never again leave port. The war was almost over and she was old. The decision had been made to scrap her. Our last Captain, Van Hoeven, told me that word had been passed to him. Mack and I had been put in for the Merchant Marine Distinguished Service Medal for our actions at Okinawa. Also, I was to be questioned by another review board about that Japanese Submarine murdering my shipmates in the Indian Ocean. That didn't fit into my plans. I knew that very soon Johnny Grady would cease to exist, this time for good. I took an inventory of my resources. I had managed to save over six thousand dollars from my pay and winnings. So I would have a good start. Now, if only the rest of my life would come together. Well, what more little surprises lay in wait for me? I fleetingly thought about the FBI. But I was confident. I began growing my beard back in Darwin. It was full now. It would take forensics experts hours of work to match the points on my face from a photograph. I doubted it could be done with that drawing.

I stood on the dock and looked at the Alma Rae for the last time. She was old, shabby, and still had a lot of battle damage visible, but she was my ship. She would always be my ship. I tried to burn the memory of her image into my brain. I would never see her again. The Roderick was my ship too. Both ships would always be part of me. These men would always be my shipmates. Captain Robeson would always be my captain. So too would Captains Van Hoeven and McIver. I had lived more in these last seven months, than in all the rest of my life combined.

Somehow, I had managed to come out of this war alive. I arrived as a hustler and opportunist, and almost lost my life in South Africa, the Indian Ocean and Okinawa. I had jeopardized my freedom. God knows how many futures I had changed. Yet I had become part of something bigger than myself. What about Charmaine? At least she had been mine for a while. I would always have her memory. I didn't expect to find her. But I would try.

I felt a hand on my shoulder. Leo was standing next to me. "Johnny, ship over with me and Mack."

"Not this time, Leo. I have things to do and can't stay at sea any longer."

"Well, how about a beer, Johnny me boy, for the road that is? Methinks we all need at least one to straighten our heads up this morning."

"OK, Leo, a short one." This was a welcome offer. I wanted to fortify my nerves, if I was going to face Charmaine's sister. We three went to the bar where we first met. I looked into the mirror behind the bar at myself. And although the face was familiar, I didn't recognize the man. I was looking at a lean, bronzed, bearded, healthy looking man with a long scar above his left eye. The face that looked back at me belonged to a man who had developed some character.

True to my declaration of having only one short one beer, actually it was five, I said my goodbyes. I left my shipmates forever, except for Mack. I asked him to follow me outside. "Mack, I'm going to change my identity very soon. I'll still see you when I can. But you mustn't ever mention to anyone, not even Leo that you ever saw Johnny Grady again. Promise?"

"I promise, Johnny!"

"Later on, I'll leave a letter for you addressed to general delivery at the post office here in San Pedro. I'll have an address by then. There will be a name on the envelope that you won't recognize, but open it anyway. It will open with the words, 'From Me.'"

"You sure I can't talk you out of this, Johnny?"

"I'm sure. I'm moving on!" I was thoughtful for a moment, and then reached into my wallet. I pulled two one hundred dollar bills and handed them to Mack. "Take these. When Leo goes broke, and you know he will; buy him a drink. Do that for me."

He took them from my hand and smiled at me. "You're one in a million, Johnny. I love you like a brother. I'm gonna miss ya."

We embraced and I moved on. Mack always let me know over the years which ship he was serving on. When he arrived in San Pedro, I always made a point of seeing him when I could.

Leo would disappear into oblivion. I liked to maintain visions of him returning to Ireland, and opening his own pub in Cork. But I knew better. He would die broke. I couldn't risk maintaining contact with him. He didn't know how to keep his mouth shut, and would have been a trail back to me.

———

I caught the red car out of San Pedro, arrived in downtown Los Angeles, and went to the storage company. There, I reclaimed my goods. Once outside, I reached into my valise and pulled out the address of Charmaine's sister. From Los Angeles, I used my interchange ticket and went on to Canoga Park. All I could think of was seeing Charmaine. She was constantly in my thoughts. I hoped we could pick up where we left off. What if she had met someone else, gotten married? What if? She probably did. Lander, she deserves better than you anyway, I mused. Suppose the FBI arrested her and I wrecked her life? We were only together a few weeks and now she must think I ditched her. Oh, let her sister still live there in Canoga Park. How will I ever find her if she doesn't? I had my sea bag slung over my shoulder, and my remaining valise in my right hand when I got off the train in Canoga Park. At the first opportunity, I hailed a taxi, handed the driver the address, and he took me on to the sister's house. I told the cab driver to wait for me as I went to the door.

"I have to keep the meter going, buddy," he said.

"No problem, sir; just stay with me. I won't be here long."

I walked up to the front door and rang the doorbell several times. A pregnant woman in her mid-twenties answered the door. She had a toddler in her arms and another holding on to her dress.

"Can I help you?" she asked.

The resemblance was strong. I knew this was Charmaine's older sister. "Hi, my name is John Winters. I've been away at sea for a long time. Can you tell me where I can find Charmaine?"

She looked disturbed. "John Winters, oh yes! I don't know if I should tell you this, but I did promise my sister. She is living with our grandparents in Wisconsin."

"Do they have a phone, mam?"

"They do! I'll write everything down for you, just like Charmaine asked me to. Please wait here."

She gave me the information. I had the cab driver take me downtown. At a public phone I dialed the operator. She finally managed to get an open line to Wisconsin, then told me how much to deposit. I heard the phone ringing and it was quickly picked up on the other end.

"Hello," came an elderly female voice with a slight Swedish sounding accent.

This must be the grandmother. "Hello, Mrs. Lund; I'm John Winters from California. May I speak to Charmaine please?"

There was silence, then in a subdued tone, she replied, "Just a moment, please; I get her for you now."

Then I heard Charmaine's sweet voice as she yelled my name. "Johnny, is it really you?" Her voice trembled with excitement.

I never felt so glad to hear a human voice as I did at that minute. I couldn't contain myself either. "It's me, honey. Can I come back to you?"

"Oh, Johnny, I cried so many tears. You just don't know. Yes! When?"

"I've been away at sea for all this time, honey. Is it OK to see you? I mean, has the FBI been looking for me or you?"

"No, Johnny. I did just what you said. I was never arrested or taken in for questioning, and I'm sure they didn't follow me. Soon after you left, I came home to live with my grandparents and have the baby here."

"Baby? What you saying Charmaine?"

"You are a papa! You have a son."

"A son! What did you name him?"

"Well, I hope you don't get mad at me, Johnny. I thought about naming him after you. But it's not easy for an unmarried girl to have a baby, and I remembered my own papa. He always loved me so, and was kind to me. I named him after my papa. Is that alright with you, Johnny? His name is Quincy."

"Quincy! Yes, Charmaine, that's just perfect with me. When was he born?"

"Two days ago, Johnny."

"Honey, you must forget the name Winters from now on. I don't go by it any longer. I'll come for you within the next two weeks, even less if I can. A couple of things must be taken care of first. Is that alright with you?"

"Yes, Johnny! What do I call you then?"

"My first name really is John. Lately, everybody calls me Johnny, just like you always did. I have a lot of stories to tell you, Charmaine."

"You really mean this, Johnny; don't you?"

"Yes, honey, and pick out the prettiest wedding dress you can find."

"I feel funny about having a church wedding after having a baby, Johnny."

"I wouldn't dream of it then, honey. We'll have it done before a justice of the peace. And you don't ever have to be ashamed about anything." I was running low on change. I had dropped most of it into the slot by now, as the operator constantly interrupted, requesting more. So I made certain of her address and we said our goodbyes. I would talk to her many times every single day, until we were reunited.

After we hung up, I knew what I had to do. I couldn't remain John Grady a moment longer. There was a paper trail. It could be covered to prove I wasn't him. I must have that just perfect identity. I had to find a man whose death didn't show up on a death certificate, and whose passing was not a matter of importance to any surviving family. I went to the main library in downtown L.A. It didn't take me long to find what I wanted there. The courthouse in Morgan County, Alabama had burned down in 1938. That was my destination.

Five days later, I thanked the editor of the Decatur Daily Newspaper in Decatur, Alabama, before leaving the building. Minutes before this, I just finished looking through old file copies from 1938. From these obituaries, I could learn who had died within a couple of days before the courthouse had burned down. There in the obituaries I saw a name that leapt back in my face as I stared at it in shock. John Bradshaw, 38, unmarried, survived by his mother and sister!

That same day I checked for these people locally. The mother had died in 1944 and the sister had moved away and disappeared. He would have been slightly more than a year older than me. It was almost a perfect match. Did he have a social security number? He did, though I had to grease a couple of palms to get it. Then I was off to Montgomery. Checking through the death certificates, there was none on file for him. At that very moment I became John Bradshaw. With this knowledge, it was an easy step getting an Alabama driver's license in the name John Bradshaw. This is strange, I thought; my son is named Quincy. He will be Quincy Bradshaw. I worked for a Quincy Bradshaw for ten years. No, it couldn't be! If it was, then his daughter Connie Randall would be my, no, it couldn't be. I put this out of my mind. Now I was on my way to Wisconsin.

Four days later, I was in my new black suit and tie looking at the Lutheran Minister who somberly regarded me. Charmaine had changed her mind about a church wedding. Her grandparents convinced her that the marriage had to be recognized by God. The minister solemnly said, "Do you, John Bradshaw, take this woman to be your lawfully wedded wife, in sickness or in health until death do you part?"

"I do."

"And do you, Charmaine Lund, take this man to be your lawfully wedded husband, in sickness or in health, until death do you part?"

"I do," she responded.

"I now pronounce you man and wife. You may kiss the bride."

I pressed Charmaine close to me and kissed her long and deep. She responded willingly and without shyness. As we separated I could see the youngest daughters of the minister giggling and whispering about Grandma Lund holding a baby.

The grandparents looked at me solemnly. They would grow to like me. I would see to that. We went back to the farmhouse where her grandmother baked us a wedding cake. We were reunited, that was all that mattered. I didn't have any strong drink that night. And I moderated my drinking behavior from then on, except on occasion when Mack was in town. And I never played the horses again, except for that occasional bet on the Derby or Triple Crown. I just happened to remember lore about famous horses of my future when I used to hang around the track. Or was it from my past? In any case, I had found something better in life.

We were in Culver City, California. It was August 15, 1945. I settled Charmaine into our modest two bedroom home on Wagner Street in Culver City. I bought it after bringing my new bride and son to Los Angeles. This was our starter home. Though I paid cash, it was still in escrow, but we were able to occupy it early. This morning we were having a late breakfast, still dressed in our bath robes while sitting at the table. I was sipping my coffee and reading the paper. VJ Day it read in big headlines.

The doorbell rang. "I'll see who it is, honey," said Charmaine. Momentarily, she came back into the kitchen, "Honey, a man just brought a letter to you. He is at the door. He says he's supposed to receive some money for it. I'm going to take my shower now, Johnny darling."

Alarmed, who would know I was here with Charmaine? "OK, baby, take your time." No one except the real estate and escrow people knew we were here. Not even her grandparents had been told. I hadn't sent a letter to Mack yet, and Charmaine's sister didn't know either. Maybe it had to do with the escrow. I walked to the front door and saw old Mr. Woodward standing before me.

"I remember you," said Mr. Woodward suddenly.

I took the letter from him; it was addressed to me John Bradshaw with no return address. Written under my name was a note. The finder of this letter will receive a one hundred dollar reward if he takes it to above named man at this address, unopened, on August 15, 1945.

"I didn't know what to make of this letter," said Mr. Woodward. "But when I found it in a box with five silver dollars in my orchard, I thought it was worth a try. Do I get the money?"

"Sure you do, Mr. Woodward; I'll be right back." I guessed I needed a cover story. I returned with the money and gave him a hundred dollar bill. "This was just a scientific experiment in honesty and human trust. It'll be part of a book someday, Mr. Woodward. Most folks just keep the five silver dollars. But those lucky few who follow the instructions to the letter get a hundred more, just like you. Congratulations!" I offered him my hand. He stared in disbelief as he took it.

He stopped looking skeptical and immediately brightened. "There's a lots o' crazy folks out there. Imagine conducting a durn fool test like that! But you folks can leave a letter like this in my orchard anytime." We said goodbye and he walked to his old truck. I watched him drive off.

I examined the outside of the letter. It had been opened and sloppily resealed. I opened it with a table knife and read the heading: Part Four of The Second Dissertation. What the

hell does this mean I wondered? Hank, could it be him? I read
through the numerous sheets of paper which didn't make much
sense in content or continuity. Old man Woodward would have
doubtlessly been bored out of his mind before he finished it.

I sat down at the table and examined the heading again:
Part Four of The Second Dissertation, Part Four of the Second,
Part Four, Dissertation. Dissertation of what, I thought. What
the! Wait a minute, there is much more to this than it appears.
There is a hidden message here. Someone is trying to signal me
from the future. It must be Hank. He is trying to send me a
message and conceal it from whoever might find it. Of course,
that had to be it. I would have to decode this. I had always been
good at solving puzzles and riddles when I was in school. I
didn't know what Hank wanted; but I was resolved to stay with
Charmaine and Quincy in this time. Hank wouldn't like that.
He might even try to reverse everything that I created here. No,
I will not let that happen. I decided I would send the valuables
through to him if we could work out the details. Hank could
have it all. I owed him that much. I would let Charmaine keep
the *Superman* Comic book. It is her favorite. Hank would have
to get another associate to work with. I hope you make it to
your future, Hank. I've found my own future in the past. I won't
give it up!

I got up, walked over to a drawer, took out a pencil and pad
of paper, and returned to the table. I began to flip these words
around in my mind, and arrange them into different patterns as I
scribbled them down. The Second Dissertation, no, couldn't be;
there never was a first dissertation. That has to be the key. Then I
realized; if I substitute word for dissertation, then I should look
at the second word. I had it; part four meant the fourth letter of

the second word. I hastily copied it down. My right hand was trembling with excitement. In but a minute longer, I realized that I must take the fourth letter of every other word of four letters or more in length. Soon I had the first word, Dear! I finished piecing together the code. Then I set about dividing up the letters into words. I read the following message.

"Dear Mr. Lander or as you are now known Mr. Bradshaw, you've come into your own and now know who I am or will be someday. You taught me this simple code when I was a boy. You instructed me to remember it when you lay there in the hospital about to die.

"Back in 1984, on your death bed, you summoned me alone and gave me this incredible story. I confess I did not believe it at the time, those instructions for meeting you at Santa Anita that fine day and what to do thereafter. I never thought any of it would ever take place. I showed up that day more out of curiosity than on a mission. But then I saw you there, in the flesh by the paddock, looking so young. The only old pictures that existed of you dated from late 1945. I knew it was you. And when you spoke, I heard my father's voice again. I had only remembered you in the flesh as being an older man. I could scarcely contain my excitement, and was convinced to follow your wishes to the letter, even to passing that tip about the next race as you instructed me. And true to your wishes, I didn't mention any of this to my mother Charmaine. She would have come to you immediately. She remained just as devoted to you after your death as she had during your life. That was a complication we couldn't risk. She never would sell that old *Superman* magazine, though it's worth a pretty penny today. Funny though, sometimes she still takes it out and looks at it. I know she's thinking of you.

"I took you under my wing to help propel you toward your destiny. When it came time for Hank to finish his device, I severed you at the firm. Your role in the world of 2007 was nearly over by then. I made my daughter Connie give you that cover story that it was her idea. And per your instructions, I gained entry into Hank's house a few days after you were supposed to return from 1945, to find out what happened to the Machine as you called it, and destroy it. On your death bed you made it clear to me. You had lost your world of the 21st century and you didn't want to risk losing this one. You told me not to be tempted by the secret of the machine. 'Son, we may cycle over and over again through eternity.' These were your exact words.

"You and Hank unleashed a strange set of events. The Einstein-Rosen Bridge floats. You can never trust those settings. No one can throw a lasso around time and ride it like a horse. Fate played a strange card into your hand. When I went inside Hank's laboratory, the machine was off. The generators were shut down. It had been running at full force until it ran out of fuel. Otherwise, nothing was wrong with it. As you instructed me, I also checked the settings. I added diesel fuel to the engines' tanks. Then I turned the generators back on, reversing the time frame from its last destination. When I opened the door to the chamber it was filled four feet deep with snow. The temperature inside was sixty degrees below zero. Wherever Hank went, I don't think he made it. He may have been trying to escape a saber-tooth tiger. I can't think of any other way that cat could have gotten into our time, if not for Hank. It was run over by an eighteen wheeler near I-5 within days. But not before it ate a few stray dogs and unlucky housecats. Its usual diet was restricted by the lack of game animals from its own time. With its short legs and slow speed, it was surviving on domestic animals."

I paused my reading, looked away and thought, poor old Hank. He only wanted a better world. A saber-tooth tiger in Southern California! What did you do Hank? I continued reading.

"That cat set off quite a stir," Quincy continued. "Tens of thousands of people set off looking in the hills of Southern California for the lost family of saber-tooth tigers. You should have heard the conservationist's plea to protect them.

"From all that I had learned from you about computers and from reading those lab notes, I used the machine as the means for this one last act of contact as you instructed me. Adjusting the settings to your original departure, I sent the box with this letter into old man Woodward's grove. It didn't land at the same time you did, but somewhere within the same range of weeks or months. We'll never know exactly when. I suppose Woodward could tell you when he found it, but it would serve no purpose. Then, I followed your instructions and destroyed Hank's machine. We couldn't risk any more social disruptions in space / time. We have to protect our own reality, the one you created. I took the magnetic polarization box, all of the journals and the hard drives out of the computers and destroyed them. Nothing there would make any sense to anyone opening the place up with these items missing.

"The substance of the machine is now destroyed. It only can be completed with your help again in 2007. Your alternate self will be born just as before in the year 1971. You mustn't try to contact him. He has to grow and develop just as you did before, or none of this may be. You are not him and he is not you. When you went back in time you created an alternate reality. You are in the era that you love the best; you told me this many times as I was growing up.

"Don't worry about your other children of these later times. They are well taken care of and will always be so. Your ex-wives were carefully guided toward their new husbands. And as I grow up through the years, you mustn't tell me any of this again until 1984.

I also looked after the well being of your old friend Mack, until he passed away in 1985, just as you had cared for him before you died. He was crying his heart out standing in the hallway before I entered your room at the hospital. I never understood what you saw in him. He always appeared to me as a rather unsavory character. But I know you've walked down roads in life that I could not begin to comprehend.

The past is always there, as is the present, and the future. You have created an anomaly in time that we will live, and live again. I look forward to growing up with you again in your coming years. Until then, goodbye, Dad! Quincy Bradshaw."

I sat there stunned as I let the letter fall to the table. Connie, Connie will be my grand-daughter. It's funny, life had some strange twists.

There were three more pages, information about stocks, and investments. Listed on these were the names of companies or commodities: Polaroid, Avon, Texas Instruments, General Motors, gold, silver, wheat, soybeans and many others. They were matched to buy and sell dates. I'll keep this part until I can commit it all to memory. Yes, Quincy, I thought; we will have a good life, and I do look forward to the future.

Charmaine walked backed into the kitchen as I separated and folded the papers. I stuffed the ones with the investments into the pocket of my robe. I would study these in detail before destroying them. I would get rid of the letter immediately. She came up to me and turned around. It was clear what she wanted, and I began zipping up her dress. I finished, stood up and walked over to the stove, turned on a burner, and held the letter to the flames.

Charmaine looked at me puzzled. "Why are you doing that Johnny? Did it upset you? Was it bad news?"

"No, Charmaine honey, just a letter from an old friend I don't expect to see for a long time to come. But you never know; I might see him any minute now." Just then we could hear Quincy crying in the bedroom.

Charmaine walked out of the kitchen and went to get him. She returned with him in her arms. "Want to go to daddy?" She handed him to me.

I gathered up Quincy in my arms and rocked him back and forth. He stopped crying. I said to him, "This is the beginning of a long time together Quincy, again and again, and I shall enjoy it each time."

Charmaine smiled, and together, we lived in a far place in time.

About the Author

Lee Cross, a graduate of California State College, is a retired locomotive engineer for the Southern Pacific Railroad, and a historian. He lives in Sparks, Nevada with his wife and two daughters.

Other books by Lee Cross:

Twelve Dreams of Laima

Printed in the United States
81142LV00001B/250-300